RAPTURE & RUIN

RAPTURE & RUIN #1

JULIA SYKES

There was no other way: I had to make Alexandra Fitzgerald suffer. I didn't have a choice. Her father had ruined my family. It was time for me to ruin *him*. If I attacked him directly, I'd bring down hell on what was left of my once-powerful family. But his daughter...

Alexandra was a much easier target.

Young. Willowy. Delicate.

Her rosy cheeks and cute little freckled nose gave her an air of innocence, but that was just a pretty lie. Ron Fitzgerald's daughter wasn't innocent. There was no way she'd managed to live under the beloved mayor's roof for twenty-one years without being tainted by his corruption. Not when she was related to that two-faced monster.

Monster. My fingers found the puckered skin that stretched too tight across my brow, obsessively tracing the damage that would never heal properly. The nerves were fried; there was a strange disconnect between my fingertips and my brain. It was like touching someone else's ruined face, not my own. It still felt foreign to me, even though nearly two years had passed since the fire.

I swallowed the acidic tang at the back of my tongue and focused on my prey, assessing my surroundings. Alexandra would come home soon, and I needed to be ready.

In my meticulous search of her home, I hadn't found any evidence of her father's criminal activities. The multimillion-dollar townhouse appeared just as cute and innocent as the young woman herself.

Deceptive. Spoiled. Frivolous.

This was a girly apartment. There was a dizzying amount of pink, for god's sake. Like everything else about Alexandra, it was a perfectly pretty cliché.

I reached out a gloved hand and snatched up a gilt-framed photo from the ornate marble mantle. My eyes adjusted to the gloom as I focused on the picture, finding Alexandra's alabaster features first. Even swathed in a shapeless black graduation gown, she seemed to shine with some inner light. Like some kind of goddamn angel with her long, flowing copper hair and luminous, peridot green eyes.

A fallen angel, but her delicate beauty was undeniable. Tempting. Cruel.

Her father's daughter.

My scar tugged on a frown, and my stomach turned as I was drawn into the photographic image of her luminous green eyes and incandescent smile. Strange, insidious warmth pulsed at the center of my chest, and my thumb traced the curve of her rosy cheek. Surely someone with that smile—like she'd never seen so much as a shadow of the world's evil—couldn't be complicit in her father's crimes.

Tension rippled through my muscles, and my grip on the frame tightened. The crack of glass beneath my thumb pierced my chest like a bullet. For several agonizing seconds, I couldn't draw in any air.

I closed my eyes and forced my lungs to expand, breathing deep. A low growl slipped between my teeth when I exhaled. I couldn't allow myself the luxury of having second thoughts. I'd come too far, suffered too much.

If the cost of my revenge was Alexandra's tears, then she would have to pay the price. No matter how innocent she appeared, those wide green eyes wouldn't change my plans for her. Before the night was through, I would make the fallen angel weep.

CHAPTER 1

ALLIE

He's a bully and a loser. Don't let him get to you. Isabel's message of solidarity lit up my screen, but I couldn't manage a nonchalant shrug and a wry smile. Not when I was alone, and I didn't have to force myself to pretend that Gavin didn't wreak havoc on the confidence I'd painstakingly built over the last three years. I thought I'd escaped his cruelty when we graduated high school, but my own personal demon had followed me to my summer internship with the U.S. Attorney's Office. Even though I'd landed my dream placement, it would've been hard enough to prove myself and escape my father's larger-than-life shadow. Gavin had turned my biggest opportunity into a nightmare.

I fiddled with my locket—a familiar comfort when I was feeling anxious—as I sent the reply to my best friend: *I won't let him get to me. I'm okay. Love you!*

Acting out of habit, I rubbed my thumb over the locket's gold surface, which was pearl-smooth from years of wear. My first initial was engraved on the front, but the back had become my personal worry stone.

I drew in a deep breath and paused at my front door. I fisted the locket, drawing on the memory of my mother's strength as I took a moment to repeat the mantra I'd adopted to bolster my confidence: *I am strong. I am independent. I can do this.*

Bullies like Gavin couldn't hurt me anymore. I wouldn't let them.

My phone chimed again. *Wanna meet up for a drink? I promised to do some posts about this cool new cantina on the socials. You can vent all about that douchebag over margaritas!*

Despite my crappy day, the knots in my stomach loosened, and a small smile tugged at my lips. I wasn't sure what I'd done to deserve a friend like Isabel, and I would always be immensely grateful for her support and loyalty. *Tomorrow night for sure!*

I slid my key into the lock and entered my apartment, beyond ready to cuddle up on my couch beneath my favorite fuzzy pink blanket. Maybe I'd pour myself a glass of pinot noir to sip while I read my new rom-com novel. Nothing relaxed me like the scent of a good book and the glide of well-worn paper beneath my fingers. If I devoured this one tonight, I'd have to go to the library on Saturday to stock up again.

Some of the tightness in my chest eased at the prospect of spending an afternoon in my favorite place in the world: the New York Public Library. I blew out a sigh and closed the door behind me, my fingers automatically finding the deadbolt lock in the darkness.

Before I could flick on the light, something warm and firm pressed against my lips, stifling my shocked gasp. A hard, masculine chest collided with my back, pushing me forward so I was pinned against the wall. Panic slashed my thoughts to ribbons, tangling my rational mind into a snarl of disjointed, primal fears. Animal instinct overtook my body as adrenaline surged through my system. My hands slapped at the wall, my palms stinging as I struggled to free myself from my attacker's hold.

He was too strong. His hand tightened over my lips to smother my scream, but he didn't have to hold me with bruising force to pin me in place. His bulky frame surrounded me, suffocated me. My chest seized; I couldn't seem to get any air into my lungs. The shadow-draped foyer spun around me, and terror was a copper tang on my tongue.

"Breathe." The growled command was punctuated by a sharp prick at the side of my neck. Insidious warmth oozed into my bloodstream, pumping through my body with each pounding beat of my heart. My muscles relaxed, and fresh oxygen flooded my lungs, enhancing the strange, alarming high that muddled my mind with each passing second. The shadows around me deepened, and I floated away into darkness.

"WAKE UP, Freckles. We need to talk."

My eyelids were far too heavy, and sleep fogged my brain. I groaned and tried to ignore the voice, but a harsh curse roused me. That deep, masculine tone set off alarm bells in my fuzzy mind, blaring at me to wake up.

A burst of instinctive fear pulsed through me, and I peeled my eyes open. I squinted into the darkness, struggling to make sense of where I was. A single, dim lightbulb hung above my head, cocooning me in a small puddle of illumination that threw the rest of the room deeper into shadow. The semicircle of floor that I could see beneath my feet was gray concrete.

My head spun, and my stomach churned. My surroundings were so foreign that they didn't seem real. This was something out of a disjointed nightmare, not real life. My flesh began to crawl, and the primal impulse to run caused my muscles to bunch beneath my skin.

The world flickered around me with each rapid pulse of my heart. The sickening effect was disorienting, but I tried to bolt anyway. My arms jerked against soft bindings, and my panic spiked. I twisted and pulled, my mind refusing to accept that my wrists were tied behind the cold metal chair that provided a rigid frame beneath my trembling body.

In my increasingly frantic struggles, a pinpoint of red light drew my attention. I barely made out the shape of a camera set up on a tripod to my right. I was being recorded.

Something stirred in the shadows, a darker shade of black. I stilled, freezing like a spooked doe.

Dread coiled in my gut as the memory of a man's hand on my mouth flooded my spinning brain. The prick at the side of my neck had been a needle, and I was lucid enough now to comprehend that my mind was still sluggish from the drugs.

The darker shadow took on the form of a towering man. He loomed over me, just at the edge of the pool of light, a nightmare shrouded in darkness. My skin pebbled with a shock of icy fear, and my belly quivered. His massive body dwarfed mine, his corded arms flexing against his tight black shirt as he crossed them over his chest. The light gleamed dimly over a mass of tousled black curls as he tipped his head back, but only the sharpest lines of his face captured any of the illumination. It rendered his face a macabre, skull-like mask.

Terror hit me like a sledgehammer to my brain, obliterating all rational thought in a burst of primal panic.

"Help!" I cried out for anyone to save me. I twisted against my restraints, but the silky binding simply slid around my wrists, securing me firmly in place. My scream tore up my throat, and the spike of abject horror magnified the dizziness from the drugs that lingered in my system. The room swirled around me, making my stomach churn. Nausea coated my shrieks in acid, and my next scream stuttered as I swallowed against the burn.

Through the unruly hair that tumbled over his brow, a flash of white indicated that my captor rolled his eyes at me. "Don't bother. Do you think I drugged you just to bring you to a place where someone could hear you scream for help?" His voice was gravelly, rough with exasperation. "We're going to have a little conversation. Screaming will only waste my time. I don't like having my time wasted." The last was a low warning, softer but somehow more terrifying than his growl.

"Who are you?" The question left my lips on a whisper. The room wouldn't stop spinning, and my stomach writhed like a nest of venomous snakes. "What do you want from me?"

"I'm Max Ferrara. And I want you to tell me all about your father's ties to the Russian Bratva."

Ferrara. My brain stuck on the name, unable to process his second statement. Through the haze of drugs and terror, it tugged at my thoughts, dragging knowledge from the back of my mind. Ice frosted over my skin, and a bone-shaking shudder wracked my body. "Please let me go," I begged on a tremulous whisper.

I didn't know this man, Max, at all, but it wasn't hard to guess why he'd kidnapped me. While my dad had served as lead prosecutor for the U.S. Attorney's Office for the Southern District of New York, he'd built the case that decimated the Italian Mafia. The Ferraras were one of five major families that he'd taken down. That'd been when I was eleven years old. Max seemed too young to have been sent to prison back then, but there was an obvious reason why he had me tied to a chair in a dark room where no one would hear me scream: revenge.

Max's teeth flashed in a savage grin. "So, you do know who I am. Good. What else did your daddy tell you about his dirty dealings? Tell me everything you know about his relationship with the Russians."

That grin sliced through any rational thought I'd managed to gather in the midst of my drugged haze. Most of his face was still hidden in shadow, but that feral flash of white teeth set off my most basic prey response. I pulled harder against the restraints that bound me, frantically trying to flee from the threat. Blood pounded in my ears, but it didn't drown out the sound of my ragged breaths. They sawed through the air around me, shredding any hope that this truly was a nightmare to ribbons.

Desperation punched my chest when I didn't manage to shift so much as an inch off the chair; the bindings weren't painful, but they held me fast.

"You don't have to hurt me," I begged in a rush. "Just let me go, and I swear I won't tell anyone about this. Please, I—"

"I'm not hurting you," he snapped, cutting off my plea. "The sooner you stop babbling, the sooner this will end. Tell me what I want to know."

His corded muscles flexed where his arms were crossed over his thick chest, a chilling reinforcement of his brute strength and my powerlessness. A shadow ticked along the harsh line of his stubble-shaded jaw, and his eerily illuminated cheekbones seemed to sharpen—like some primal, fearsome beast that dwelled in darkness.

I squeezed my eyes shut, willing my head to stop spinning. Everything was surreal and sickening. If my world could just go back to normal, if only this were a nightmare and I could wake up…

"Focus, Freckles." A sharp snap directly in front of my face jolted through my entire body like a thunderclap. "The Russians," the beast prompted. "Tell me about your father and the Russians."

"Russians?" I parroted the word in a squeak, compelled to say something—anything at all—if it would appease my captor.

A flash of white as he rolled his eyes again. "Yes, Russians. The Bratva. I know your father must've told you about his dealings. Daddy dearest obviously trusts his precious princess. He's texted three times in the last half hour." A rectangle of bright light blurred across my vision as he waved my phone at me.

Hope sparked in my chest. Daddy would worry if I didn't answer his texts. He would come to my apartment looking for me. As the mayor of New

York, he could mobilize an army of law enforcement to find me.

My captor seemed to read my thoughts. "He won't find you," he informed me with cold certainty. "I already used your thumbprint to unlock your phone and reply. You communicate with too many emojis, by the way. Anyone with half a brain could figure out what to say to keep your father from worrying. Your security is shit, Freckles."

"Don't call me that," I snapped without thinking. The familiar, cruel nickname hit me with a gut punch of reflexive anger. I'd felt this powerless, help-less rage far too many times before. The impotent fury made my insides burn, but the familiar searing heat was far more comfortable than the bone-chilling terror of being held captive.

His head tipped back, causing shadows to pool into the deep hollows beneath his cheekbones. What little I'd been able to make out of his features melted into darkness, leaving me staring into that awful, skull-like mask.

I shrank into the unyielding metal chair, with-ering beneath the weight of his macabre glower. My fingers trembled, and I reflexively closed my fists to hide the sign of weakness. Bullies fed off my weak-ness. That's what made tormenting me fun for them.

My heart pounded erratically against my ribcage,

and the room lurched around me. Past trauma and current, horrific reality were blending together. Still under the influence of whatever had been in that syringe, I could no longer differentiate this hostage scenario from awful memories of being terrorized by my worst bullies. Panic clawed at my brain, and years of learned coping mechanisms clicked into place to protect me from the worst of the abuse that was to come. I couldn't allow innate fear responses to betray how terrified I was. That would only encourage my tormentor to continue toying with me.

"You'd be better off answering my questions instead of arguing with me, Alexandra." He emphasized my name, and it was somehow worse than the mocking nickname. His low, quiet tone resonated through the dimly lit room, caressing my skin in a silky-smooth threat. He said my name like he knew all my darkest secrets, ones that were buried so deep, even I wasn't aware of them yet. "You know about your father's connection to the Bratva. And you're going to tell me everything."

I couldn't fathom knowing anything terrible enough to warrant the heavy condemnation in his tone, but he spoke with such absolute certainty that for a moment, I questioned my sanity.

I shook my head to clear it. The movement made

my thoughts slosh in my brain. "I don't know what you're talking about." My tongue was too thick in my mouth, and my words slurred slightly.

Don't show weakness. I swallowed and tried again. "Let me go."

He muttered a low curse. "I shouldn't have dosed you so much. You're even more delicate than you look."

I'm not delicate! The snappish, kneejerk retort was at the tip of my tongue, but I pressed my lips together to lock it inside. I couldn't allow him to see how much he was riling me.

Weak. Skinny. Ugly. You look like a little boy. My bullies' words echoed in my head, rolling around inside my skull and heightening my nausea.

"Tell me what I want to know, and you can go home. You're staying right here until you talk, Freckles."

"I told you not to call me that!" I burst out before I could stop myself.

"I'll call you whatever I want. You're the one tied to a chair in my basement. You don't get to make demands, *Freckles.*" He placed extra emphasis on the mocking nickname, twisting the knife. I caught another flash of white teeth as he bared a cruel smile at me.

"You're a bully," I seethed in a moment of absolute clarity, cleaving to my righteous, familiar rage. It seared away the worst of my debilitating terror. "You think you can scare me into telling you what you want to hear. I don't know anything about any Russians. I don't know if you're insane or if you're just getting off on terrorizing me. But you're a bully, and I've dealt with bullies before. You won't get anything out of me."

So far, Max hadn't physically hurt me to get me to talk. In fact, he'd barely touched me at all. I knew his type. He wanted my fear. I wouldn't give him the satisfaction, and I wouldn't give him any nasty lies he could use against my father. He'd put that camera there for a reason: he wanted to record my testimony.

"You think I'm just a bully." His voice went cold and flat, and I realized he'd been almost conversational until now. A chill danced over my skin, making my flesh pebble and my fine hairs stand on end.

I'd been wrong. This man wasn't toying with me. He wasn't playing games.

He ran a hand through the dark curls that fell over his brow, pushing his hair back so his eyes flashed through the gloom. His long fingers wrapped around the arms of the chair at either side of me, and he surged forward into my personal space.

I couldn't stifle my horrified shriek when his snarling face stopped within inches of my own.

"I'm not a bully," he growled. "I am a monster out of your worst nightmares." Full lips twisted on a grimace, teeth snapping on each menacing word. The ferocious expression contorted his features, and a true beast snarled in my face. The sparse light overhead caught in the craggy, ruined flesh around his right eye, casting rippling shadows that formed a grotesque mask. The dark pools in the hollows beneath his high cheekbones were more skull-like than ever.

I jerked back on instinct, and the movement caused the world to swirl around me. The horrible face wavered and twisted before my eyes. My heart leapt into my throat, blocking my ability to breathe. I gasped for air, and something hot and wet spilled down my cheeks.

A harsh, inhuman sound grated across my senses, like claws scraping down my spine. My hands shook in their bonds, and a sob wracked my body.

Suddenly, the terrible face was gone. My tormentor slid back into the shadows, melting into the darkness. "Do you understand what you're dealing with now?" The words were strangely rough, as though forced through a mouthful of gravel. "Tell me about your father's ties to the Bratva. I know he worked with them to destroy my family. You're going to give me proof. I want details, names. I want every scrap of information in your pretty head. You will tell me. You're not leaving here until you do."

"I-I don't... I w-won't..." My protests wavered on little hitching breaths. I couldn't find the air to tell him that I didn't know what he was talking about, and that I wouldn't simply say whatever insanity he wanted to hear.

I couldn't conceal my fear anymore. Not when the burst of terror and swirl of drugs left my head spinning. This nightmare couldn't be real. That monster couldn't be real. Nothing he said made any sense, and despite my horror, something deep inside me knew that I couldn't lie to appease him. I couldn't betray my father like that, no matter how scared I was.

A low curse hissed from the shadows. "Breathe, Alexandra. I'm not going to hurt you." Another curse, softer this time. "But I will keep you here until you talk."

"I don't have anything to say to you," I managed faintly. I closed my eyes to block out the spinning room. It barely helped.

A heavy sigh ghosted around me. His boots stomped against the concrete floor, retreating to the far corner of the basement. I squinted just in time for a flash of bright light to sear my vision. I recognized the sound of a fridge closing as I squeezed my eyes shut tight.

His footsteps approached me, and I shrank back into the unyielding chair. When his body heat kissed my chilled skin, I peeked up at him, dread a lead weight in my stomach. I didn't want to look into the monster's face again, but instinct urged me to keep my eyes on the threat.

Mercifully, he remained mostly cloaked in shadow, sparing me his terrible snarl. His hand was illuminated by the light above me as he extended a bottle of water toward my lips. "Here. You need to hydrate."

I turned my face away, fearful of drinking anything he offered me. He'd already drugged me once.

Another sigh, roughened by an exasperated growl. "It's just water. I want you to sober up. You're useless to me like this."

"Then you shouldn't have drugged me." The bitter words popped out before I could think better of antagonizing him.

Something had softened in him since I'd started weeping. The palpable menace that'd pulsed from his huge body ever since I'd woken up seemed to have dissipated. He was still towering over me, still cloaked in darkness, but the shadows concealing his beastly appearance now seemed merciful rather than frightening. He was granting me a reprieve from his terrifying snarl.

I'm not going to hurt you. His low promise played through my mind. He hadn't hurt me so far. Even the binding around my wrists was smooth and silky, too soft to chafe my skin, no matter how much I twisted and pulled. Now, he was offering me water.

I suddenly became aware of the cotton-wool dryness in my mouth and the sandpaper itch behind my eyes. I couldn't think clearly through the haze that still blanketed my mind. His words and actions didn't make any sense to me, but I had a better chance of figuring my way out of this awful scenario if I could sober up.

I glanced sidelong at the water bottle, and my mouth went desert dry. My lips were chapped, and I couldn't manage to moisten them with my tongue.

He released an annoyed grunt and withdrew the offered water. A soft sound of protest left my chest as I watched him take a sip. I could still barely see his features, but as he lowered the bottle, his free hand tangled in his curls, tugging his hair down over the terrible scar around his eye.

I am a monster out of your worst nightmares. Was that how he thought of himself? He was trying to scare me into giving him false testimony, but he hadn't laid a hand on me. Did he think his disfigurement was disturbing enough to make me talk?

"Here." He extended his hand again, offering the water. "Now you know it's not drugged. Happy?"

"Not remotely," I muttered, more of my fear ebbing away. I really was thirsty, and my head was starting to pound.

"Just drink the damn water," he grumbled, pressing the cool bottle to my mouth. He waited for me to part my lips and accept what he offered rather than roughly forcing it down my throat.

I opened my mouth and tipped my head back slightly, allowing the water to soothe my parched throat. A low groan eased from my chest as the cool liquid wet my tongue and lips. I hadn't realized how miserably dehydrated I was until I took that first sip.

Some of the water spilled down my chin and splashed onto my chest, but I didn't care. I greedily gulped down everything he offered me, my fears about being drugged allayed by the fact that he'd taken a drink from the same bottle first.

When I'd drained half of it, he pulled away, allowing me to draw in a shuddering breath. It felt good to breathe now that my mouth was no longer painfully dry, so I didn't even register any fear when his thumb brushed away droplets of water that clung to my lower lip. The touch was gentle, despite the slight rasp of a callous over my soft skin.

A light shiver raced over my body, and he pulled his hand away, moving slowly enough not to spook me. The careful way he handled me increased my confidence that he wouldn't harm me. I blinked several times, clearing the cobwebs from my mind.

He'd said his last name was Ferrara. He'd said that my father had destroyed his family. That was true; my father had sent many of his family members to jail, and they'd lost everything. But Max was young, probably only a few years older than me. Maybe the version of his family history that he'd been told was different from the hard reality that they alone were responsible for their crimes. This stuff about the Bratva had to be a complete fabrication.

And with that awful scar, it wasn't hard to guess that life hadn't been kind to him. My own bullies had been bad enough, taunting me for my boyish figure and pale, freckled complexion. I could only imagine how much worse people would've treated him because of his disfigurement.

"How's your head?" he asked, the words a reluctant rumble.

"Better." I bit my lip, but it was too late to take back my reflexive answer. He wanted to know if my head was clearer so I could answer his insane questions.

"Okay, let's try this again," he began, his voice almost gentle. "Your father worked with the Bratva to bring my family down ten years ago. He took money from Russian oligarchs to advance his political aspirations, and in exchange, they helped him become the hero of New York: the man who brought down the Italian Mafia. I already know it, so there's no point pretending otherwise. What I don't have is proof. That's why you're here. Once you tell me everything you know, I'll take you home unharmed. Don't be stupid, Alexandra. Remember who you're dealing with."

He pulled farther back into the shadows, tugging his hair over his brow again. Something squeezed in my chest. *I am a monster out of your worst nightmares.*

Max's questions were crazy, but maybe he wasn't entirely sane. His actions were certainly those of a madman: drugging and kidnapping me. Right now, I needed help, but maybe he needed help too.

"It's Allie," I offered, hoping to relate to him on a more personal level. He'd been calling me *Freckles* before he realized it was a trigger for me. It occurred to me that maybe he'd been trying to keep his emotional distance. There was an edgy, desperate energy about Max. He badly wanted to believe what he was saying about my father, and he craved my confirmation.

He took another step back, his massive frame swelling with tension. "I already told you I'll call you whatever I want." I didn't miss the fact that the barbed statement wasn't followed by a mocking nickname. "You want to go home, don't you? Talk." The last was a snapped command.

But I wasn't quite as terrified of his volatility anymore. If I could just appeal to his humanity, he might calm down long enough to see reason.

"You're wrong," I said quietly. "My father didn't do any of those things. I do know a little about your family, and if you suffered because of my dad's case against them, I'm sorry. You couldn't have had anything to do with their crimes back then. But whatever you've been told about my father is a lie. He's a good man, and I won't betray him by giving you a recording of those lies. I can't say what you want me to say because it's not true."

A growl slid from the shadows. "You must know something. You're working for the U.S. Attorney's Office, just like your father. I don't believe that he has you following in his footsteps in total ignorance. Daddy would've told his princess how the world really works, what you need to get ahead in life."

I peered at him, my eyes straining to see his

features through the gloom. His scarred appearance had horrified me before, but I'd been woozy from the drugs, and he'd been snarling in my face. Now, I wished I could read him better. He used the shadows as a shield between us, protecting himself as much as they were meant to intimidate me.

"What do you expect to gain from all this?" I lifted my shoulders to indicate my bound state. "Even if I tell you what you want to hear, what will that accomplish? You said you won't hurt me, and I think I believe you. But I can't betray my father with lies that will destroy his character and reputation. I love him, and I won't do that."

Purpose firmed my resolve, and the terror that'd left a metallic tang on my tongue finally receded. Primal panic no longer clawed at my mind. I could reason my way out of this.

"You should be scared of me." His voice went cold and flat again, just like it had before he'd surged into my personal space and told me he was a monster.

But he hadn't touched me then, and I thought he was bluffing again now.

I hoped.

"Well, I'm not," I said with more bravado than I felt. "I think you're hurting. I think you've been through something awful, and it's pushed you to this point. I can help you, Max."

He crossed his arms over his chest, his muscles bulging and flexing as though resisting some physical strain. "You can help me by confessing your father's sins. You want to know what I want out of all this? Why I risked kidnapping the mayor's daughter? I want leverage. I want your father to know that he can't fuck with my family ever again."

His voice shook with rage and something darker. He had suffered because of my father's actions. His family had been sent to prison, and he'd been forced to grow up without them. That didn't make my dad a bad person, but Max wouldn't see it that way.

"Listen, Max." I intentionally used his name, and he flinched as though I'd struck him. "I can't give you what you want. I don't know who told you those outrageous lies about my father, but they're not true. Just let me go home, and I won't tell anyone about this." He scoffed, but I continued on. "I'm serious. You haven't hurt me, but I can tell that you have been hurt. You think you're somehow defending your family by doing this, but I'll defend my family, too. You have nothing to gain by keeping me here, and the longer you do, the greater the chance that my father will launch a manhunt to locate me."

He was silent for several long seconds, his head cocked to the side as he considered me. "You really don't know anything, do you?" he finally said, his voice heavy with some emotion I couldn't quite identify. Regret? Despair?

"There's nothing to know," I replied evenly. "My father has nothing to do with the Bratva. I am sorry for whatever you've been through." I meant every word. Max had terrorized me, but he'd clearly suffered through some terrible things if he'd been pushed to this mad scheme.

"Don't pity me," he barked. "You're the one tied to a chair in my basement."

As though I needed reminding.

"I won't tell anyone about this," I promised again, my voice clear and calm. I did pity him. It gave me no pleasure, but I felt sorry for this broken, scarred man. He was so desperate to defend his family that he believed my father was a villain. In his mind, it was the only way to vindicate and protect them.

"No, you won't," he agreed, his promise darker than my own. He stepped into the light, dropping to one knee as his powerful arms bracketed me once again. His big hands fisted around the metal chair at either side of me, knuckles white with strain. The overhead light cast craggy shadows beneath the scarred flesh around his eye. This time, I barely flinched when he snarled in my face. He couldn't help that he'd been permanently scarred by some horrific injury. The mark of his pain wasn't a threat to me.

"I won't hurt you, but I have no problem hurting your father," he seethed. "If you tell anyone about this, he will pay the price." His eyes glinted with an almost fanatical light, and the fine lines around his mouth drew deep with strain. Max hated my father, and I fully believed that he wouldn't hesitate to follow through on his malicious promise.

Even once he let me go, Max's rage wouldn't ease. This threat to my father wouldn't disappear unless someone addressed Max's pain and misguided beliefs.

Let me help you. The entreaty teased at the tip of my tongue, but I swallowed it back.

Manic energy pulsed from his huge frame, a dangerous vibration over my flesh. He'd risked everything to capture me, and he'd gotten nothing for his efforts. He was far too volatile at this moment for me to show any more softness or pity. He was on the verge of releasing me, and I didn't dare breathe a word that might make him change his mind.

"I won't say anything to anyone," I swore, willing him to believe me. "I won't put my family at risk." Daddy was the only family I had left. Max seemed to understand loyalty—it was what had driven him to kidnap me.

He huffed out a breath, and the tension eased from his harsh features. For the first time, I got a good look at his face. If it weren't for the horrific scar, Max would've been devastatingly handsome with those high cheekbones, sensual mouth, and a jawline sharp enough to cut. I could only imagine the verbal torment he must've endured for his appearance.

His dark eyes dropped from mine, and long, thick lashes fanned his left cheek. Whatever had scarred him—fire?—didn't seem to have injured the right eye itself, but it'd scored the flesh on his brow and cheekbone. The puckered skin was obscured by the thick black curls he allowed to grow in an unruly mass to conceal the worst of the damage.

"I'll hold you to that," he murmured, a low warning. One hand slipped into his pocket, and my stomach dropped when he uncapped the syringe.

"What are you doing?" I jerked and twisted, but the silky restraints held firm. I barely felt the sting of the needle sliding into my arm, but horror mingled with the warmth of the drugs as they oozed into my system. My body began to relax, and my eyelids became lead weights.

My heart slammed into my ribcage in a renewed burst of terror. The loss of control was horrifying, and while my mind still whirred, I registered how completely vulnerable the drugs made me.

"Please…" I whispered, even though it was too late to stop him from doing whatever he wanted.

He shushed me gently. "Don't be afraid. I'm taking you home."

The basement dissolved around me, his reassurances following me down into darkness.

CHAPTER 2

ALLIE

My head pounded, and my eyelids itched like sandpaper. I groaned and rolled over. The mattress disappeared beneath me, and I jolted awake when my butt hit the floor. For a second, I flailed, my bedroom swimming around me.

No. Not my bedroom. I pressed a hand to my forehead, trying to alleviate the worst of the ache that throbbed against my skull with each of my rapid heartbeats.

I was sprawled on the floral rug in my living room. I must've fallen asleep on the couch, cuddled up beneath my favorite fuzzy pink blanket. But I didn't remember…

I gasped, and everything came into sharp focus as I went on high alert. Frantically, my eyes searched the room, fearful that my captor still lurked in the shadows.

But there weren't any shadows. Bright sunlight streamed through the large bay window, flooding the room with natural light. I wasn't in that awful basement. I wasn't bound to a chair while a monster interrogated me.

The terrible, beastly mask filled my mind, and I clutched a hand over my racing heart as I struggled to draw in oxygen.

My eyes swept the room a second time. And a third.

The monster was nowhere in sight. For a moment, I doubted that the horrific experience had even been real. It felt impossible now that I was back in my cheery townhouse, surrounded by the safety of my own home and bathed in warm sunshine.

But I recognized my pounding headache and scratchy eyelids all too well. These were the exact symptoms that'd assailed me when I'd first awoken in that basement and found myself trapped in a nightmare.

My fingers rubbed my wrists, checking for restraints that weren't there. Not even the faintest bruise marked my skin where he'd bound me to that rigid metal chair.

I sucked in a deep breath, remembering the softness of the bindings.

I'm not going to hurt you. Don't be afraid. Even though he'd terrorized me, Max had gone out of his way to make sure I was unharmed by the experience. He'd wanted to scare me into talking, but he hadn't wanted to hurt me.

I recalled the cool sensation of the water he'd offered me, soothing my parched throat and alleviating the worst of my headache. Suddenly, I was desperately thirsty.

I struggled to my feet, swaying slightly at the lingering dizziness from the drugs.

Yes, the nightmare had definitely been real, and I was still feeling the lingering effects.

I stumbled toward my kitchen, quickly grabbing a glass from the cabinet and filling it with chilled water from my fridge. I moaned when the cool liquid slid over my tongue and down my scratchy throat.

Max might not have wanted to hurt me, but the aftereffects of those drugs were worse than the most wicked hangover of my life.

Despite the nauseating waves of heat that rolled just beneath my skin, my flesh pebbled with an echo of the bone-deep chill that'd settled over me in that basement. I rubbed my arms, hugging myself tight.

The back of my neck prickled, and I shot a wary glance around my brightly lit kitchen. I couldn't shake the fear that'd taken root in my psyche, keeping me on high alert for danger that seemed to have evaporated in the morning sunlight.

Moving with slow caution, I tiptoed around my entire apartment, checking every corner for signs of my assailant.

Not a single one of my belongings was out of place. It was as though Max was a ghost, not the corporeal monster who'd bound me to a chair and asked me insane questions about my father and the Russian Bratva.

I am a monster out of your worst nightmares. A shiver raced over my skin as his snarled words played through my mind.

I took a deep breath and focused on the memory of his face, not when he'd snarled at me, but later, just before he'd let me go. His features had softened, and his eyes had dropped from mine as though he couldn't bear to look at me.

Or he couldn't bear my eyes on him.

He'd warned me that he was a monster, but at that moment, he'd been a damaged man tormented by regret. His mad scheme had come to nothing, and his despair had been palpable.

Did he regret kidnapping me? Or was he devastated by the fact that I hadn't confirmed the awful lies he'd said about my father?

I jolted at the thought of my dad. *I won't hurt you, but I have no problem hurting your father,* Max had threatened.

A fresh spike of panic sent me rushing back into the living room, searching for my phone. It lay on my glass coffee table, right beside where I'd slept on my couch.

I barely registered a small swell of relief that Max hadn't violated the privacy of my bedroom before I snatched up my phone. My jaw dropped when the screen lit up. The Notes app was open, and if I'd been tempted to think last night had been a terrible dream, the confirmation of awful reality was emblazoned on my phone: *Your security is shit. Set a passcode. I'm not the only monster out here.*

My skin crawled, and my eyes darted around the room once again. I rubbed at the back of my neck, trying to alleviate the maddening prickling warning that I was being watched.

Immediately, I opened my security settings and changed them so that my phone unlocked with a six-digit passcode rather than my thumbprint. The iron band around my chest loosened slightly once it was done; Max wouldn't be able to break into my texts again. No one would be able to access my private messages.

I hastily exited my settings and opened up my messenger, frantically scrolling through the last four texts to my father.

My mouth twisted in a scowl when I noted a couple of one-word responses accompanied by multiple emojis. Max had been able to hold off my father's concerns with a few smiley faces. My stomach lurched at the sudden, undeniable knowledge that Max had been able to abduct me without anyone realizing I was missing. How long would it have taken for Daddy to suspect that something was wrong?

My boss probably would've reached out to him when I didn't show up to my internship this morning.

My internship! I checked the time, and a thrill of panic fluttered through me. I was going to be late for work!

I shook my head, immediately rejecting the ridiculousness of my concern. I had far worse things to worry about.

Like my father's safety. Max's threat against him rang through my mind like an alarm bell.

My fingers found my dad's contact details and

connected before I could take another breath. It only rang twice before he answered.

"Morning, sweetheart." His voice was warm with pleasant surprise. Not so much as a tense thread of fear for my safety.

My stomach sank. Max truly had orchestrated the perfect crime. Despite the fact that my father had spent the last ten years being overprotective in the extreme, he'd had no idea that I'd been kidnapped last night. My attempts to keep him at a distance so I could live my own adult life had allowed my captor to easily dismiss my dad's potential concern.

"Daddy!" I couldn't help the hitch on his name. "Are you okay?"

"Yeah, I'm fine." His voice suddenly quickened with alarm. "Are you okay?"

"Yes!" I squeaked, the lie popping out immediately as I remembered the second part of Max's threat: *If you tell anyone about this, he will pay the price.*

"Allie." His tone dropped to the stern, warning tone that always made me squirm. "Is something wrong?"

"No, no." I forced the denial through my constricted throat. "Everything's fine." I scrambled for an explanation for my obvious distress. "Um, I'm just running late for work, and I'm worried that it'll damage the review that Mr. Callahan will send to my university at the end of the summer. What should I say to fix this?"

"It's not like you to be late." More heavy disapproval. "What happened?"

"I, ah… I went out with Isabel last night. She's an influencer, you know. Social media posts on new restaurants and stuff. I, um, had too many margaritas and overslept." I winced, bracing myself for his censure. Anything was better than telling him the truth and putting his safety at risk, but his long sigh still made my stomach drop. "I know it's totally unprofessional," I rushed to continue. "I swear I won't do it again. Please tell me how I can mitigate the damage?" The last lilted on a high-pitched question, my voice going thin with strain.

"Maybe you should come stay at the house for a little while. I knew it was too soon for you to move out on your own."

"No!" My refusal was vehement and immediate. I'd been suffocating in that house. I loved my dad, but he'd watched my every move for the last decade. He loved me so much that he'd smothered me, especially after Mom died. He'd only allowed me the freedom to move out on my own two months ago.

"No, I want to stay at my new place," I pleaded. "This won't happen again. I just wanted your advice. Please?"

I wanted to hear your voice. I wanted to know that you're okay.

I locked those worries behind my pursed lips. I didn't dare breathe a word of my kidnapping to my father. Not with Max's threats against him still echoing clearly in my mind.

Another heavy sigh. "Okay, sweetheart. You don't have to come home. You're young, and it's normal for you to make mistakes. Just make sure you learn from this one."

"Yeah, totally," I rushed to respond. "I'll never do this again. Trust me, I feel awful." Mentally and physically.

"I can call Mike," he offered.

"No!" I burst out again, my cheeks already burning with mortification. I'd be humiliated if Daddy called my boss to smooth things over. This summer was about proving myself, and I'd rather stagger into work drunk than have him call Mr. Callahan, his friend and former colleague.

"No, but thanks," I added, struggling for calm. "This is my mess, and I need to handle it on my own. I was just hoping you could give me some advice. I'll take responsibility for running late, but I can't tell Mr. Callahan that I'm hungover. That's unprofessional."

Despite the fact that my hangover was a

complete fabrication, a lead weight of guilt sank in my chest. I always took responsibility for my mistakes, and even though my condition this morning wasn't at all my fault, I still felt the emotional gut punch of failure.

"In this case, a little white lie is okay," Daddy reassured me, most of the disapproval ebbing from his tone now that I'd thoroughly admitted my supposed mistake. "Mike will probably be able to figure out the gist of the situation, but you're right. It's unprofessional to say you're hungover. Just say you're not feeling one-hundred-percent, but offer to work late to catch up on whatever you miss this morning. Assure him that you'll stay until you meet all your responsibilities and then some. Mike isn't unreasonable. He was once twenty-one years old, too. We've all been there."

I huffed out the breath I didn't realize I was holding. My dad was safe, and I was forgiven for my false transgression. "Thanks, Daddy. I'll do that."

"All right, princess." The warmth returned to his tone. "Thanks for trusting me to give you advice about this. I'm glad you know you can call me with these kinds of problems. I'll always be here for you."

My throat tightened, and my eyes burned. "I know. I love you, Daddy."

"I love you too, sweetheart. Now, get moving.

You don't want to be later than you already are. And drink plenty of water."

"I will," I promised.

When I ended the call, my legs turned to jelly, and I sank down onto my couch. I buried my face in my hands, pressing my palms against my wet lashes to hold in the flood of tears that threatened to overwhelm me. I didn't have time to fall to pieces. My reputation was on the line, and I couldn't tell anyone the terrible truth about what had happened to me last night.

A text alert chimed, drawing an alarmed yelp from my chest. I grabbed at my phone like a lifeline, searching for something normal to hold on to.

A message from Isabel illuminated my screen, following up on her invite to the cantina. Had it only been twelve hours ago that she'd tried to cheer me up after my crappy day with Gavin?

I closed my eyes on a low groan. I would have to face my bully again today. My nerves were frazzled, and I wasn't sure how I was going to make my excuses to my boss without tearing up. I hated disappointing people. I would have to endure Mr. Callahan's censure and Gavin's cruelty, all while pretending I hadn't been tied to a chair in a basement and terrorized overnight.

For a moment, it was too much. A swell of ugly,

dark emotions surged from deep within me, leaving my chest on a harsh sob. My body convulsed, all my residual terror overwhelming me.

Max's face, twisted with rage and pain, filled my mind. He'd been terrifying in his fury, but his pain had been my salvation. I'd been right to think that he'd suffered something awful. Appealing to his humanity had saved me.

I gulped in several gasping breaths, my head spinning slightly from the rush of oxygen.

I'd survived being drugged and kidnapped. I could survive Mr. Callahan's disappointment and Gavin's bullying. I would survive it, because I didn't have a choice.

Max would hurt my dad if I dared to unburden myself of the awful things that'd happened to me last night.

I squared my shoulders and swallowed hard, crushing all my tumultuous emotions into a tight ball and locking them away. Swiping the tears from my cheeks, I typed a quick message to Isabel, promising to meet up at the cantina after work tonight. Somehow, I would get through today. I would protect my father, no matter what. He was the only family I had left, and I would do anything to keep him safe.

I got to my feet and moved toward the bedroom

on shaky legs, forcing myself to take each step. I had to try to be presentable for work, even if I was late.

I am strong. I am independent. I can do this. My mantra felt pathetically insufficient to cope with the aftermath of my abduction, but it was all I had. I repeated it over and over, willing the words to be true.

CHAPTER 3

MAX

*W*arm blood splattered my cheek, leaving little sizzling marks that stoked the fiery hatred inside me. The man's agonized screams didn't bother me; he was less than human, and he didn't deserve any compassion. He was Bratva scum, a drug dealer who beat his whores.

I welcomed the warmth of his blood on my face. The more dead Russians, the better. And if he had to suffer first, that was fine with me.

I'd seen what these animals were capable of. I'd been forced to witness their depravity firsthand when I was little more than a child.

My mother's screams were a distant echo in the back of my mind. I slammed the door shut on those horrific memories, loathing the weakness that came over me whenever I fell prey to the past. I needed my body carefully under my control. Symptoms of primal fear couldn't touch me. Not when I had a job to do. Not when my sadistic cousins were watching me with suspicion.

"What?" I demanded when Paulie glanced sidelong at me for the dozenth time this morning. It wasn't like him to be distracted when he had the opportunity to torture someone.

I made men bleed when it was necessary; my cousins reveled in it.

"Where were you earlier?" Paulie's head canted to the side, and he dropped his red-painted hands as he focused on me.

His twin, John, eagerly took his place. The meaty thud of his fist punching bloody flesh echoed dully through the warehouse where we'd strung up our enemy.

I lifted my chin, my cold gaze clashing with his merciless black eyes. "None of your fucking business."

"I called you three times to help us pick up this bastard." He landed a casual punch to the man's wounded side, and the Russian howled in pain. "John and I had to bring him in on our own, and you didn't get here until dawn." A nasty little smile twisted his thin lips. "You know how your father hates when you shirk your responsibilities. I should tell him about this."

I curled my mouth in a sneer, swallowing the flutter of panic in my chest. "Father hates little bitches who rat out their own. I'm his son. Who do you think he'll side with?"

John released a low laugh between punches, half-listening to our conversation. "You're a disgrace, and your old man knows it. We all know it. I don't know why we even expected you to show your ugly face this morning. You don't understand the first thing about family loyalty or responsibility."

I stifled a growl, unwilling to let them see how hard that particular blow landed. Everything I'd done last night had been to prove my loyalty. I'd ignored their calls because I'd been questioning Alexandra. I'd planned to scare her into divulge her father's secrets. Once Ron Fitzgerald knew that I had testimony of his crimes and could leak it at any time, he wouldn't dare come after my family ever again. We would be free to reclaim what we'd lost.

And it would all be because of me. I would be a worthy heir. A worthy son.

My cousins would have no part in it. This was my mission. The glory would be mine and mine alone.

So, I couldn't tell them where I'd been or why I'd ignored their calls.

"I'm here now." My fingers tightened around the hilt of the knife that hung casually at my side, an extension of my arm. "I know my duty. Better than you two ever will."

Duty had been burned into me. It seared my soul with purpose, right alongside my rage and hatred.

Paulie snickered, his anvil-hard features twisting into a vindictive mask. "We didn't have to have our sense of duty beaten into us. You think you're more valuable just because you're the heir. But one more fuckup, and your old man will probably let us put you in the ground."

In a blink, I slammed into him. The metal wall boomed when his heavy body collided with it, reverberating around the dank, cavernous space. My knife was at his throat before he could draw another breath. The only language my deranged cousins understood was violence.

"Do not threaten me." I hissed each word, my blood boiling in my veins. "I've had a shitty night, and I'm all out of patience. Give me one more reason to slit your throat." He opened his mouth to speak, so I pressed my blade just deep enough to draw a bead of blood. "My father likes you, but even he knows that rabid dogs have to be put down."

"Get away from my brother." John's deep voice rumbled with rage and a touch of fear. I could kill Paulie in a heartbeat, and he didn't dare do anything that might make my hand slip. Not when my knife was pressing into his twin's artery.

"Threaten me again, and I'll end you." I raised my voice, addressing both of them, but I didn't take my gaze off Paulie. The whites of his eyes were huge around his dark irises, and his bulky body was utterly still.

"We have work to do," I reminded them, impatience edging the words. I had to get the fuck out of here. Morning light peeked between the cracks in the huge metal doors, melting away the most oppressive darkness that clung to the corners of the massive warehouse. The rays of warm sunshine singed my insides with the burning need to get back to Alexandra.

If she went to the cops...

I pushed away from Paulie with a warning growl, freeing him from my knife. He gasped in a breath and rubbed his neck, swiping away the blood I'd drawn.

"Asshole," John spat.

I nodded at the bleeding Russian. "Who's shirking their responsibilities now?" I challenged, prompting them to get back to work.

Paulie stalked over to the man, who let out a garbled plea through broken teeth just before my cousin's fist slammed into his jaw.

John addressed the Russian, but he kept a wary eye on me. "Tell us who your boss is. We want a name."

We knew the man was Bratva. He'd dared to move his product in what had once been our territory—before most of my family had been sent to prison by Ron Fitzgerald. We would take back what was ours, inch by bloody inch. This man's gory death would be a warning. We'd dump his body once we were done. But we wanted intel first.

Impatience was an itch beneath my skin. We'd been at this for nearly two hours, and the man hadn't talked. He was either too loyal or too scared of his bosses to share information.

And I needed to leave. I had to watch Alexandra and make sure she didn't break her word. If she called the police, I'd be fucked.

I won't tell anyone about this. Her desperate promise echoed through my mind, and the memory of her wide, fearful green eyes cut at me.

My stomach turned. *Innocent.* Alexandra had been completely innocent, and I'd terrorized her.

Kidnapping her had been an act of desperation. I'd been after her father for nearly two years, and I'd gotten nowhere. I'd taken Alexandra to get the leverage I needed against him, but my mad plan had come to nothing.

My ruined face alone had been horrific enough to make her scream, and her terrified sobs had ripped at my chest as keenly as a serrated blade.

I rolled my shoulders, seeking to loosen the tension in my muscles. My body was coiled tight with the pressing need to get back to her. I wouldn't touch her ever again, but I had to watch her today. I had to make sure she didn't go to the cops or tell her daddy about what the monster had done to her in the dead of night.

I can tell that you have been hurt. Her strange words played through my mind, tingeing my thoughts with a hot mixture of shame and anger. Despite everything I'd done to her, she'd pitied me.

She'd *pitied* me.

I allowed myself to be consumed by my anger, the familiar heat of rage lending me strength.

Fuck this. I was done dicking around with this Russian bastard. He wasn't going to say anything, and I had more important places to be.

I shouldered my cousins aside and slashed my knife in a smooth arc, slitting the man's throat. Hot blood sprayed my face and coated my hand.

If Alexandra could see me now, she wouldn't dare pity me. She'd scream and sob in terror.

My stomach twisted.

"What the fuck?" John demanded. "He didn't talk yet."

"He wasn't going to," I said coldly. "Dump him somewhere his friends will find him."

Paulie cussed at me, but I ignored him.

I turned my back on the gore, leaving my sadistic relatives to clean up the mess. No matter if I was disgraced, I was still the heir. And they wouldn't dare question me again. Not today, at least.

Once I got what I needed on Fitzgerald, no one would ever question my loyalty again. I would be worthy, respected.

I just had to ensure that Alexandra didn't put me behind bars first.

CHAPTER 4

ALLIE

"**Y**ou're late, Freckles."

I jolted and gasped for breath as Max's furious, twisted face filled my vision.

"Jesus, you look like shit."

I recognized Gavin's voice. My bully had said the mocking nickname, not my fierce captor. I wasn't in that dank basement; I was in the U.S. Attorney's Office, rushing to see my boss so that I could make my feeble excuses for being late.

I automatically curled my hands to fists to hide the fact that my fingers were trembling from the sudden rush of residual terror. *Don't show weakness.*

With effort, I forced my lungs to expand on a deep breath and relaxed my stiff shoulders. I schooled my face to a carefully neutral expression and turned to face my longtime tormentor.

"Good morning, Gavin." I greeted him coolly, as though he was just another colleague and he hadn't insulted me in the middle of the office.

I glanced around, the quick darting of my eyes betraying my nervousness. Had anyone overheard him? It would've been obvious to anyone paying attention that I'd rushed into work almost an hour late, but the prospect of being ridiculed by my bully in front of senior staff made my face heat with the first blush of mortification.

Damn it, now my cheeks were pink. I'd learned to mostly control my body language when enduring Gavin's cruelty, but I'd never been able to master the flush of my alabaster skin. And after looking in the mirror this morning, I knew it was even paler than usual. Dark circles smudged beneath my eyes, and my freckles were more pronounced than ever, covering my face like splattered mud. I'd been in such a rush to get out the door that I'd barely taken time to put on minimal makeup. Over the years, my carrot-red hair had darkened to a merciful shade of copper, but my lashes and brows were still a soft ginger color. Without makeup to define those hated features, I looked like a washed-out mess.

My appearance didn't even begin to mirror the

extent to which I felt like a mess on the inside. My mind was a fear-addled wreck, jittery thoughts skittering across my consciousness. I'd barely managed to collect myself enough to walk with my head held high: a shadow of professionalism. Gavin sensed my distress like a shark scenting blood in the water. I hadn't even made it to Mr. Callahan's office to apologize in person, and my tormentor had already pounced.

"I have work to do." I tried for a frosty tone, and to my credit, I managed to lift my chin and look him squarely in his navy-blue eyes. They danced with cruel amusement, and his pearly white grin tilted at one corner. With his dark blond hair perfectly styled and his impeccably tailored suit absolutely wrinkle-free, I appeared even more haggard standing in his vicinity.

"Looks like someone started the weekend early. I didn't think you were a party girl, but coming into work hungover?" He clicked his tongue in mock disappointment. "You surprise me, Freckles. You were always so lame in high school." His eyes raked down my body, scoring a stinging trail everywhere his judgmental gaze landed. "You know, I was actually starting to think you were kind of hot. Turns out you need a pound of makeup to look halfway decent. You always were a pale freak."

I glanced around again, anxiety getting the better of me. No one seemed to be paying us any attention, and my bully spoke in a low tone that was meant just for me. People bustled past, but they were far more concerned with their caseload than my private war with Gavin.

A war that I was losing.

Badly.

To my horror, a lump formed in my throat, and my eyes burned. *No no no!* I couldn't cry in front of Gavin.

But after the terrible events that'd taken place in less than twenty-four hours, all my emotional strength had been tapped out.

His grin turned nasty, splitting his handsome features into something monstrous. "Aw, are you going to cry? I knew you weren't cut out for this internship. No way did a mouse like you qualify on merit. Do you know how hard I had to work to get this gig? And your daddy probably placed one phone call to his buddy Callahan and ensured your placement here."

"Oh, shut up!" I snapped, completely losing my tenuous composure. "You're not some disadvantaged underdog. You're a spoiled brat, and I wouldn't be surprised if *your* dad was the one to grease the wheels to secure your placement. He probably couldn't stand the prospect of everyone realizing that his precious son is a stupid, entitled douchebag."

"Miss Fitzgerald." Mr. Callahan's voice cracked through my tirade like a whip. "I'll see you in my office."

All the blood drained from my face, and my stomach dropped to the floor.

Oh god, oh god, oh god. My boss had heard me berating a colleague. I'd called Gavin a *douchebag* right in front of him. No one had heard my bully needling me, but he'd riled me enough that I'd raised my voice in impotent fury. I'd been desperate to hurt him like he'd been hurting me, but I'd only given him what he wanted.

His malicious grin remained fixed in place, his eyes flashing with triumph. He stepped in close, making sure I felt his intimidating presence. At six-foot one, he towered over my five-foot four frame.

Memories of when he'd used that size to his advantage assailed me. At our elite private school, he had been the popular golden boy and the ringleader of my numerous tormentors. I'd been an obvious target: the awkward kid with a dead mom and a famous dad who didn't quite know how to raise a girl. Ever since we'd both landed the same internship, it'd taken all my willpower to resist Gavin's renewed cruelty. Today, I'd finally cracked.

I hated that he could make me feel like this again. I'd worked so hard to overcome this weakness, but my awful ordeal with Max had made me far too fragile this morning.

"Enjoy getting fired," Gavin said in a low, almost intimate whisper. He waited until a tremor raced over my skin before turning on his heel and strolling away like he hadn't just ripped me to shreds.

"Allie," Mr. Callahan prompted, already halfway to his office.

I cringed and followed him on leaden legs, feeling as though I was headed for the gallows. I was so getting fired. That office door would close behind me, and I would be scolded before being told to pack up my desk. All my dreams and determination to make my own way in the world crumbled inside my chest.

Somehow, I made it into his office. The soft click of the door closing behind me clanged through my body like a prison cell locking me in and sealing my fate. My internship was over. My reputation was destroyed.

I sank my teeth into my lower lip to stop it from quivering. I stared at a spot on the worn blue carpet, unable to meet Mr. Callahan's disappointed gaze.

"Is Gavin bothering you?" he asked.

I blinked, sure I must be misinterpreting his

gentle tone. He sounded almost concerned, but that couldn't be right. I'd just insulted a coworker in the middle of the office.

"You can tell me," he said, still sounding bafflingly reassuring. His gray eyes were soft and warm, and the fine lines around his salt and pepper moustache drew deeper with worry. "I doubt you called him a douchebag if he didn't deserve it." His lips quirked up at the corners, as though he was fighting a smile.

Then he turned suddenly grim. "If Mr. McCrae is being inappropriate with you, tell me now, and I'll handle it. I don't tolerate workplace harassment."

A confession teased the tip of my tongue. My life would be so much easier if Gavin were fired. I wouldn't have to see him at all. We didn't go to the same university; he'd chosen Harvard, whereas I'd had enough of hyper-elite schools and ruthless rivalries. It was just bad luck that our families ran in the same circles, and he'd gone for the same prestigious legal internship that I'd applied for.

I swallowed hard and shook my head, refusing the lifeline Mr. Callahan offered. Gavin's dad was one of my father's biggest political supporters and donors. I couldn't let my personal weakness damage such an important relationship. My dad loved being mayor, helping the people of New York. I wouldn't do anything that might sour his connections.

"No, sir. Gavin's not harassing me. We just had a disagreement, and I..." My throat went tight, trying to hold in the false admission that I was unfit to work this morning because of my own carelessness. I squared my shoulders and forced myself to continue. "I'm not feeling one-hundred-percent today. I'm sorry I behaved unprofessionally. And I'm so sorry that I was late. I'll put in whatever hours are necessary to get caught up. Please let me know what I can do to make this right."

My tone barely wavered by the end, and my back was straight. There. The worst was over. I'd taken responsibility for my supposed personal failings. Now I just had to withstand Mr. Callahan's judgment. At least he didn't seem to be in the mood to fire me, so I kept a tiny spark of hope flickering in my chest.

His lips thinned, and I suppressed the urge to squirm beneath his scrutiny. Then, to my shock, he placed a warm hand on my shoulder in an undeniably reassuring gesture. "You can talk to me, Allie. You're not in trouble. I already know Gavin's no angel. You were right, by the way: his father made a call to my superiors. I wouldn't have approved his placement if my hand hadn't been forced. You earned your right to be here. He didn't. Never think otherwise."

"You heard that?" I squeaked, mortified that my boss had been privy to more of the awful conversation than I'd realized.

His hand squeezed gently, offering paternal comfort that I never would've expected from the wickedly clever and infamously tough prosecutor. "Relax, Allie," he soothed. "I'm not angry with you. I wish I could give that little shit a piece of my mind, too." He beamed at me, appearing almost proud. "But don't tell anyone I said that."

"I won't," I breathed, quick to promise him anything that would keep him smiling rather than yelling at me for my failings. I cleared my throat, struggling to maintain professionalism. "But I am sorry for being late today. Please let me know what I can do to make it up to you, Mr. Callahan."

"It's Mike." He corrected me with a wink. "I'm not as scary as you seem to think, but I have to admit I'm a little flattered that you find me so intimidating."

"Well, your record speaks for itself," I gushed, marveling that one of my personal heroes was being so casual with me. "My dad's always said that you're one of the smartest people he's ever known. I referenced your work on the Kassel case in my law school application essay. Totally inspiring."

Mr. Callahan—Mike—laughed, a rich sound that warmed my insides and chased away the last of the chill in my bones. "Now I'm definitely flattered. Where did you apply?"

"Columbia. I won't find out if I'm admitted until the fall, but I applied early. It's my first-choice law school."

"Your dad's alma mater." His voice was rich with approval, and I soaked it in. "I'm sure he's very proud of you. Based on your work ethic and GPA, I'm sure you'll successfully follow in his footsteps."

I fiddled with my locket, slightly anxious but pleased at the praise. "I'm not planning on going into politics," I admitted. Everyone thought I was trying to emulate my father—and I supposed I was choosing a similar path for my education and career choice. But that was about proving that I was capable and strong. My future would be very different. "I want to stay in Law. I want to make a difference."

Mike's brows rose. "You want to be a prosecutor?"

I nodded. "I plan to go pro bono after I establish my career for a few years. I want to help people."

"You're considering pro bono?" He seemed surprised and a little impressed.

I basked in his approval. "Yes. I want to help women who have been victims of assault. I want to help them get justice."

My heart burned with familiar purpose as I said the words, and my fingers traced the outline of my locket. My mother had been my personal hero, and when it'd come time to choose a volunteering position as part of my high school curriculum, I'd followed her example: I'd spent four years helping out at a local women's shelter. Once I got to college, I started pushing for women's rights in my political initiatives with the Young Democrats.

I knew what evil men were capable of, and I would do everything I could to empower and protect vulnerable women.

Mike noted my fierce expression and smiled. "You might not want to admit it, but you are your father's daughter. He's a good person, too."

I flushed at the compliment, warmth flooding my chest. I could hardly believe the turn this conversation had taken. I wasn't going to be fired. And Gavin really hadn't earned his place here. I should've known that he only leveled that underhanded accusation at me because it was his own reality. But I'd been so frazzled that I'd shrieked childish insults instead of calmly issuing a retort.

Mike gave my shoulder one last reassuring squeeze before slowly drawing away. "I'm glad to see you smiling again. Don't let that douchebag get to you."

My jaw dropped when he echoed my insult to Gavin, and he chuckled. "You don't have to look so shocked. I'm only human. I do have a sense of humor." Some of the levity dropped from his tone, and I stood straighter under his suddenly stern bearing. "Tell me if he's bothering you, Allie. I mean it. I'd love to have an excuse to fire his ass."

My mouth opened and closed a few times before I settled on nodding mutely. This whole situation had gone better than I ever could've dreamed. Not only was I not fired, but Mr. Callahan had invited me to be on a first-name basis with him. He'd called Gavin on his shit.

"Thanks, Mr. Callahan," I finally managed.

"Mike," he corrected me, still stern.

I offered him an almost giddy smile, still in disbelief that this was really happening. "Mike."

He beamed. "Okay, go get to work. No need to stay late. Just get as much done as you can before five. A young woman like you should have some fun on a Friday night. Don't stay here too long."

"I won't," I promised, even though that was a white lie. I would stay as long as necessary to catch up on what I'd missed this morning. "Thank you."

He gave me a nod, dismissing me with another warm smile.

I walked back out into the hall like I was floating

on a cloud. This day had been such an emotional rollercoaster that my head was spinning. For the next few merciful hours, I finally found the mental fortitude to shove all thoughts of Max and Gavin from my mind.

CHAPTER 5

I glanced out the cantina window, and my heart stopped. A terribly familiar, hulking figure leaned casually against the side of a bus stop across the street. The vibrant city lights shone brightly above him, gleaming over his unruly mass of black curls and well-worn leather jacket. Shadows pooled beneath his hair, concealing his brow and eyes. His high cheekbones were just as harshly defined as I remembered: sharp and feral.

Max Ferrara. He was watching me, stalking me. I'd foolishly thought he'd let me go, but he wasn't willing to back off and leave me in peace. Was he waiting to get me alone again? Would he kidnap me and hold me hostage this time?

"Hey, babe." Isabel brushed her hand over mine, and I jolted at the casual show of support. "That asshole can't bother you anymore. Not today, and not next week."

For a moment, I froze. How did she know about Max? I hadn't breathed a word about my abduction or my volatile captor. The dark secret was a rabid beast in my throat, desperate to claw its way out of me. But if I unburdened myself to my friends, I'd put my father at risk. I'd sworn to Max that I wouldn't tell anyone what he'd done to me, and I intended to keep that promise until the day I died.

Isabel couldn't know about Max. I hadn't slipped up and revealed anything about my ordeal. Had I?

"You said your boss wants to fire him, right?" she prompted when I didn't respond right away.

A bus stopped in front of the dark figure across the street, hiding him from view. When it pulled away, he was gone.

I ran shaky fingers through my hair. *Gavin. She's talking about Gavin.*

"Right," I said faintly, struggling to direct my focus back on my friends. The man in the leather jacket wasn't necessarily Max. Lots of men had curly black hair and high cheekbones. And had aloof, menacing vibes that pulsed from their massive bodies, making passersby skirt to the side to avoid their dangerous aura.

"I still think you should tell Mr. Callahan the

truth," Charlie said, her soft Georgia drawl taking on that stern, grown-up tone. She was only three months older than me, but she was by far the most mature of the four of us.

"Mr. Callahan?" Davis snickered. "Don't you mean *Mike*? Allie, you're totally the teacher's pet. And I agree. Make him fire that douchebag, Gavin. Sounds like you have your boss wrapped around your little finger."

Isabel squeezed my hand. "Of course she does. Allie is awesome like that." She released me so she could raise her margarita, tipping it toward me in celebration of my supposed awesomeness. "You've got this, babe. You're the total package: smart, sweet, and gorgeous. No wonder Gavin is a jealous little bitch."

"Jealous?" Davis' brows rose to his light blond hair, his sea green eyes going wide. His chest puffed out with indignation, making his lithe dancer's body appear bulkier than usual. "More like horny. He totally wishes he could get in your pants, honey."

"Davis!" Charlie squawked. "Gavin is terrible. He's not getting anywhere near Allie's pants."

"I didn't say he was." Davis waved his margarita, a little bit of tequila-tinged liquid spilling over the side of the glass with his vehement gesture. "Just that he wants to. Remember how he got that mean girl to send you the note in high school?" he asked me.

As though I could forget.

When I was thirteen, Gavin had gotten a popular girl to pass me a note from him, saying that he liked me. Despite his previous cruelties, I'd been desperate for social validation, and my heart had leapt.

A low groan left my chest. "Please don't remind me. He loudly and scathingly rejected me in the cafeteria, making sure the whole school witnessed my humiliation."

Davis leaned in closer to me, his voice dropping low like he was telling a secret. "Trust me, I was the bullied gay kid in high school. The meanest bullies are always the ones who want to fuck you. They know they can't without damaging their popularity, so they take out their sexual frustration on you. Little bitches."

"Little dick energy," Isabel amended with a sage nod.

I shook my head. "You guys didn't know me in high school. I was a total mess." A wry smile tugged at my lips, and I finally released most of the tension that knotted my stomach. My friends were amazing, and I'd so much rather bask in their camaraderie than spend my evening on edge, looking for signs of Max in every shadow.

"You would've called me a *fashion disaster*," I told Isabel. My bestie was so cool that sometimes I was in total awe that we were even friends. With her lustrous black hair, dark eyes, and bronze complexion, Isabel was nothing short of a goddess. She had over a hundred thousand followers on social media for a reason. *Star power* didn't even begin to cover how brightly she sparkled. There was no doubt in my mind that her recent leading role in an off-Broadway play would start her path to A-list celebrity status.

Charlie slung an arm over my shoulder. "That's why you have me." She lifted a warm tortilla chip and waved it like an imaginary magic wand. "I'm your fashion fairy godmother."

I laughed for the first time in what felt like days, shedding more of the terrible, lingering fear that'd burdened me. "And I'm eternally grateful."

Charlie had been in my English Literature class during my freshman year, and I'd helped tutor her when she struggled with the material. She was a curvy blonde bombshell and a Fashion major, and at first, I'd been intimidated by her chic style. But she'd taken me under her wing and shown me the ways of Ted Baker and Bobbi Brown. Now, I was nearly as polished as she was, thanks to the fact that she took being my personal stylist seriously. I'd be sartorially lost without her.

"You can't help it that your dad's clueless when it comes to girly stuff," Isabel interjected in her signature protective tone. The oldest of five siblings, she came from a large, tight-knit Puerto Rican family, and she took her role as big sister seriously. "He didn't know how to help you style yourself when you were a teenager. That's why you have us now."

I released a grateful sigh. "And I don't know what I'd do without you." Sometimes, it still seemed surreal that these wonderful people actually liked me and wanted to spend time with me. I wasn't sure what I'd done to deserve their love and loyalty, but we'd become as close as family over the last three years.

"You would be just fine without us, because you're awesome," Davis reminded me. Everyone seemed to be on the cheer-up-Allie train this evening, and after the awful things I'd experienced in the last twenty-four hours, I didn't feel like protesting their overly lavish praise.

Instead, I took a deep gulp of my margarita and rubbed my locket, my cheeks flushing at the intense compliments they were piling on. "Thanks," I murmured, still not used to accepting so much enthusiastic kindness, even though years had passed since my nightmarish high school experiences. "But I really wouldn't be fine without you. I love you guys so much."

"We love you too, babe," Isabel promised as Davis and Charlie echoed their agreement. She glanced around and made eye contact with our server, who hastened toward our table, his eyes wide on Isabel. I wasn't sure if his awestruck glow was due to her stunning, natural beauty or if he was a social media fan. As soon as he reached us, Isabel ordered another round of margaritas, and he rushed off to the bar.

"We need more tequila," she announced, her ochre gaze fixing on me. "You deserve a night to unwind. You work too hard, and you've had a hell of a week."

"Maybe if we get enough drinks in you, we can convince you to get Gavin fired. You're seriously not thinking clearly on this one," Davis said decisively. "If I had the chance to crush one of my bullies' dreams, I'd totally do it."

"That's because you're a badass," Isabel approved. "Allie, you should take notes."

I tugged on a lock of my hair and shifted in my seat, slightly uncomfortable despite their loving support. "You guys, I can't get him fired. His dad is one of my father's biggest donors."

"You think Gavin's dad would withdraw his

support if you made sure his son gets what he deserves?" Charlie's delicately arched brows drew together in outrage, her electric blue eyes sparking. "That's bullshit."

I shrugged. "That's politics."

"Well, it's still bullshit," Davis asserted. "But your dad needs to be mayor, so I guess that means the douchebag gets a pass." His mouth took on a glum twist.

Davis practically hero-worshipped my dad because of his progressive policies. We'd first met at a rally for the Young Democrats at our university, and we'd clicked immediately; we were passionate about the same political initiatives. Davis had totally freaked when he found out I was Ron Fitzgerald's daughter. It was a minor miracle that he'd gotten past being starstruck and started being frank with me—a real friend.

He and Isabel were already close, both self-professed theater nerds from the same high school. So he'd introduced us, and I'd introduced them to Charlie, and here we were: an eclectic little family.

The next round of margaritas arrived, along with complimentary tableside guacamole. Dutifully, Isabel gave the server a megawatt smile and snapped some pictures with her phone. He gushed that he loved her posts and was one of her thousands of followers. She was as gracious and humble as ever; Isabel never took her budding success for granted.

Once he left, she turned her camera on us. "I need some candids," she announced. "Come on, Allie. Look like you're happy to see us." She shot me an exaggerated pout. "Don't let that douchebag ruin your night."

I tucked my hair behind my ear and ducked my head, wishing I could hide under the table until this part was over. Overcoming my shyness to pose for Isabel's pictures was a challenge on my best days. And this was so not one of them.

"It's not Gavin," I said truthfully. I couldn't tell them about what'd happened with Max, but I could at least share a little of the anxiety that'd haunted me all day. "I, um, overslept and didn't have time to do my makeup this morning. Then I worked late and came straight here. My blouse is wrinkled, and my skin looks like crap. I didn't even put on mascara."

"You don't need mascara," Charlie admonished gently. "And you have gorgeous, clear skin. I never would've taught you my makeup tips and tricks if I'd known you would rely on them so much. You look beautiful no matter what. Trust me, no one will be focusing on your wrinkled blouse."

Davis shot me a sympathetic look. "Gavin really did a number on your self-esteem today, didn't he?

Look, I've seen pics of you from high school, and yeah, your style was a train wreck."

"Davis!" Isabel hissed, going into protective big sister mode. "Not cool."

He waved her off, keeping me fixed in a no-nonsense green gaze. "We all go through an awkward phase. I used to wear acid washed double denim. *Double denim,* Allie. It was tragic. But you're fabulous, and now that you're all grown up, you look just as fabulous on the outside. Don't let that bully dull your shine. He doesn't deserve one more second of your time."

"Accurate," Charlie agreed, tugging me close in a one-armed hug. Despite my lingering insecurities, my lips curved in a smile. I loved my friends so damn much.

Isabel snapped a pic and grinned at me, unrepentant. "Perfect candid for the socials. You two look adorable."

"Excuse me!" Davis said, affronted at being left out.

Isabel captured an image of his indignant glower and snickered. She showed it to him, and he groaned. "No, don't post that. I look constipated."

She pulled him close and took a selfie of the two of them as a loud, genuine laugh burst from my chest. Their antics cleared away the last of the storm clouds that'd hung over me all day. Isabel beamed at me and snapped another pic of me laughing.

"Stunning," she declared.

I lifted my margarita to my lips and took a long drink. It was past time for me to unwind, and I didn't have to go into work tomorrow. I had freaking earned this salt-laced tequila.

I eased back into my seat and sipped at my beverage, basking in the pleasant warmth of the alcohol and the effervescent energy of my friends. Nothing bad could touch me when I was surrounded by their love. Not Gavin's bullying and not the haunting memory of Max's snarling face. For a few blissful hours, I was perfectly content.

I should've known it was too good to last. When I stumbled off the bus and began to close the short distance to my apartment, I stopped dead in my tracks. A man with tousled black hair and a leather jacket lurked directly across the street, half hidden in shadow.

My nightmare had followed me home. My initial instincts had been right: Max was stalking me.

CHAPTER 6

ALLIE

*I*ncandescent rage flooded my body in a pulse of reckless strength. I'd been through too much, and seeing the bastard stalking me caused something to snap inside my mind. The adrenaline rush sharpened my senses so that my full focus centered on Max.

Ever since he'd first materialized from the shadows in my apartment and slipped a needle into my neck, my instinct had been to try to run away. Well, that instinct hadn't saved me from being tormented. It hadn't saved my dad from Max's deranged, sinister plans. Proof of his menacing resolve radiated from his hulking, shadowy form.

He intended to continue to victimize me. I'd allowed one bully to shred me today. Now, I'd been buoyed by my besties and more than a little tequila.

My blood ran hot in my veins, and my fingers curled to fists at my sides. I'd be damned if I let another man crush my spirit. Especially since my dad's safety was at risk.

When Gavin had taunted me this morning, I hadn't been able to find the strength to stand up for myself. But Max wasn't solely a threat to me, and I sure as hell would protect my family.

Max thought he could loom in the shadows and wait to get me alone again? Screw that. He'd made the mistake of letting me glimpse him in public. It was probably part of some sick intimidation mind game, but it would backfire on him now.

My street wasn't particularly busy, but we were both out in the open. If I confronted him now, he wouldn't dare try anything with potential witnesses around. Max didn't want to be caught. He'd let me go on the condition that I keep his little abduction-and-interrogation session secret. That meant he wouldn't risk getting the cops called on him if I screamed for help where people could actually hear my pleas.

I would tell him in no uncertain terms that my father had nothing to do with the Bratva. He would get the picture and back off. His vendetta was rooted in lies, and once he accepted that, he'd leave me and my dad alone.

Rage, alcohol, and a determination to protect my dad fueled me with purpose, harnessing my full focus. Peripheral concerns like Max's mental instability or his massive muscles became white noise at the back of my mind. At that moment, it seemed completely logical that my only option was to confront the son of an infamous mobster: the deranged, damaged man who'd held me captive in his basement mere hours ago.

Before I could formulate any second thoughts, I squared my shoulders and turned to face Max. My chin tilted in challenge, and I spared only a brief glance at the road before taking the first purposeful step toward him. I stomped across the pavement, timing my movements to dodge the light traffic that traversed my neighborhood at this time of night.

Max's body tensed, and his head jerked back as though I'd sucker punched him. I was close enough now to see his mouth drop open in shock, and I caught the flash of widened eyes through his tangle of curls.

That's right, douchebag, I thought with grim satisfaction. *I am not a victim. Be afraid.*

I am strong. I am independent. I can do this.

A tingling giddiness washed through me as I repeated my mantra of self-empowerment. The heady sensation raced from my brain to my fingers and toes. My knees wobbled at the strange, dangerous rush, and I missed a step on my high heel. My ankle turned, and the ground rushed up to meet me.

Several sensory inputs slammed into me all at once: jagged pain cracked into my knees, a car horn blared, and a harsh curse snapped through the night air. Suddenly, strong arms closed around me, hauling me up and out of the way of oncoming traffic. For a second, shock rendered me motionless. The logical burst of fear at being trapped in my ferocious captor's arms didn't register; survival instincts made my fingers bite into his corded arms, pressing into his leather jacket hard enough to bruise as I clung on tight.

The car horn blared again, followed by more cursing from a different masculine voice. A tremor wracked my body, adrenaline spiking higher than ever. My nerves were jittery, my mind a tangled mess.

"Fuck off," Max snapped back at the enraged driver who was currently cussing me out. He pulled me closer, and I realized my legs shook so badly that I couldn't put any weight on my feet. Max's strong grip was the only thing holding me upright.

An engine revved, and the person who'd almost hit me with his car sped off, leaving me alone with the mercurial man who'd drugged and kidnapped me. The man I'd been about to confront when I'd fallen in the street and nearly been killed.

The two different traumas warred for my emotional attention—almost getting run over and being held captive by Max.

My body seemed more preoccupied with the almost getting run over thing, because I couldn't seem to unlatch my fingers from his bulging biceps.

Keeping his firm grip around my waist, Max hauled me farther away from the street and set me down on a bus stop bench. My hands were still locked on his arms when he released me and dropped to his knees.

"Are you insane?" he demanded, his voice taking on the rough, furious tone that'd frightened me so much last night. The beast was snarling at me, practically vibrating with anger.

But I was running on pure adrenaline, and my entire being was too wrapped up in the residual horror of almost getting flattened to focus on the threat Max should pose.

"Are you?" I snapped back, still riding the strange, reckless high that'd claimed me when I'd first started stomping toward him with grim purpose. "You're *stalking me*," I reminded him. As though either of us could forget it.

A flash of white through those dark curls as he rolled his eyes at me. "I was making sure you kept your promise not to tell anyone about last night. I'm not a threat to you."

"Well, you're sure doing a good job of acting threatening."

He huffed out an exasperated breath, and his long fingers skated down my leg, starting just beneath the hem of my modest pencil skirt. Rough callouses tingled over my pebbled flesh, my every nerve alive from the adrenaline dump as he caressed my knee before working his way downward.

"What are you doing?" My voice hitched slightly on the demand, probably shaking from residual fear.

"Checking to make sure you didn't break your damn ankle, Bambi," he rumbled, applying light pressure to the delicate bones beneath the thin strap of my designer heels. His big hands were shockingly gentle, touching me the way one might handle an injured bird.

"Bambi?" I repeated, breathless from the shock of having my massive captor handle me with such aching care, as though his thick fingers might break me if he applied the barest pressure.

"Yep," he declared decisively, his full focus on my ankle rather than my face. "You have those big, innocent eyes; long, unsteady legs; and no sense of self-preservation."

"I don't want you to call me Bambi." Did I sound petulant? Damn it, I was supposed to be incensed and intimidating, not quivering and weak while my captor tended to my potential injuries. Almost getting hit by a car had really messed up my priorities.

"Well, I don't want you to risk your pretty neck recklessly confronting me, but here we are," he retorted, his voice still edged with anger even as his touch remained featherlight on my hypersensitive skin. "What the hell were you thinking, approaching a man like me? Don't you understand how fucking dangerous that is?" His fingers dusted my scraped knees, and I hissed at the sting. "You'll need to clean these up," he said more gently. "Come on. Let's get you home."

"You're not coming home with me!" I declared hotly, immediately rebelling at the idea of having the beast in my private sanctuary. "You're not coming anywhere near me!"

His eyes finally met mine, and that black brow over his left eye arched as he stared at me pointedly: *I'm near you right now.* He didn't have to say the words aloud for my cheeks to heat with something between chagrin and indignation. His hands were still on my legs, his huge palms nearly engulfing my calves.

"I'm not going to hurt you," he swore, low and serious. The streetlights caught in his black eyes, flickering over them like white-hot flames. Even obscured by his tousled hair, his right eye flashed through the darkness, keen with the fervor of his promise. "But you need to stop being so reckless. I'm not the only monster out here, and your father is neck-deep in organized crime. They'll know who you are."

A half-mad laugh burst from my chest as the absurdity of his warning fizzed through me, bubbling alongside my lingering adrenaline. "Reckless? *You* think *I'm* reckless? You freaking kidnapped and interrogated the mayor's daughter. You're lucky you're not behind bars right now."

His light hold on my calves firmed ever so slightly as his massive body tensed. "I thought we'd reached an agreement about going to the cops, Alexandra." That soft, dangerous tone sent a thrill through my belly, but I didn't cower. I'd learned that when it came to me, Max was all bark and no bite.

"We did, and I'll keep my promise," I assured him. I calmed, purpose settling over me as I remembered why I'd decided to approach him in the first place. "But you have to leave my dad alone. I know you think he's a bad person, but you're wrong. When I saw you tonight, I wondered if you planned to kidnap me again, but I chose to confront you because I have to convince you that my father is innocent. You're obviously not ready to drop this, and I can't leave him in danger like that."

He released a heavy sigh, the tension leaving his muscles. "Listen, Bambi—"

"It's Allie," I interjected. I was so over the diminutive nicknames, even if *Bambi* wasn't triggering like *Freckles*. It was still irritating.

"Right." Another eye roll. He seemed to do that a lot. He didn't take me seriously; he didn't take terrorizing an innocent woman seriously. Max was either insane, or he didn't possess a normal moral compass. It was infuriating as hell.

"You're naïve," he continued in that maddeningly dismissive cadence. "I get that now. Your daddy's kept you in the dark about the reality of his climb to power. How do you think he affords your fancy designer clothes and even fancier education? Where do you think all that money came from?"

"He wrote a book," I countered, struggling to remain collected when I wanted so badly to shake him. *Naïve?* What an arrogant asshole.

I finally peeled my fingers from his corded biceps and crossed my arms over my chest. He didn't so much as flinch from my suddenly prickly demeanor. Instead, that single black brow crept higher, and he remained resolutely in my personal space. His hands were still on my legs. I was hyperaware of the heat of his long fingers wrapping around my shins, holding me with that careful but masculine grip.

I focused on the heat of my indignation to distract myself from the disconcerting warmth of his touch. "My dad's book spent weeks on the *New York Times* best-sellers list. And he does all sorts of speaking engagements. He gets paid for those. He's accomplished a lot, and his time and insight are valuable. He loves New York and cares about the people who live here more than anything. It's not a crime for him to be compensated for his knowledge and years of public service. You have him all wrong."

"*Public service.*" Max's full lips twisted in a sneer, the defined lines of his face sharpening into the harsh mask that'd terrified me in that basement. He didn't surge toward me with that awful snarl again, but he didn't back down, either. His body heat kissed my skin as he growled, "You mean good deeds like destroying my family?"

I swallowed hard, drawing on all my willpower not to cringe away from that terrible, beastly scowl. "Your family isn't innocent, Max." I spoke gently to avoid provoking him, but his jaw still ticked when I said his name. "They bear sole responsibility for the consequences they faced. I can understand why they might've told you a different version of what happened, but it's just not true." I paused, choosing my next words carefully. "I don't know what you've been through, but I can tell that you've suffered. But whatever happened to you doesn't—"

"Stop talking." I didn't miss the warning that roughened the command. "You don't know anything about me, and you don't know anything about your father. That's why I let you go. But I don't have to sit here and listen to your pitying bullshit."

Despite his unnerving tone, I pressed on, desperate to protect my dad from his misguided vengeance. "Max, please. You don't have to—"

"I said stop talking!" he barked, his massive body swelling with barely contained rage. He still knelt before me, but he suddenly towered over me, his hulking frame crowding me back against the bus stop bench. He leaned in close, so I could feel the heat of his hissed demand whisper across my cheeks. "Don't bother pleading with me. You think I'll forget all about your father's sins if you just blink those big, doe eyes at me? You might be innocent, but he's not. If you want to stay ignorant, that's your choice, but don't keep repeating the lies your daddy fed you about how fucking virtuous he is. Not to me. Not ever. Understand?"

I couldn't stop the shiver that raced across my suddenly chilled skin, and my fingers clamped around my locket for comfort. My teeth sank into my lower lip to hide its trembling, but I managed a shaky nod. My eyes burned as the remembered trauma of being held captive settled over me like a suffocating weight. Maybe I had been a fool to approach Max so fearlessly.

I am a monster out of your worst nightmares.

The man looming over me wasn't safe. He was unstable, and it didn't matter if something terrible had happened to him to drive him to this madness. He might not be pure evil, but he was still dangerous, no matter if he'd been hurt.

A low grunt caught in his chest, and he abruptly shoved away from me. "I said I wouldn't hurt you, and I meant it," he muttered, mercifully releasing me from his intense black stare.

He pushed to his feet, then glanced down at me. Reflexively, I hugged my arms protectively over my chest and shrank into the bench at my back.

His lips pinched as though he'd bitten into something sour. "You don't have to be afraid of me, Bambi. I'm sorry if I scared you."

"It's Allie," I whispered, hating the way he dehumanized me with the dismissive nicknames.

A shadow danced over his tight jaw, and he shook his head sharply. "You're still bleeding," he rumbled. "You should get home and clean up. Come on. I'll walk you to your door."

He held out a big hand, and I cringed away. His fingers clenched to a fist as he slowly withdrew the offered support.

When I didn't move for several tense seconds, he spoke again. "It's late. I'm not leaving you out here on your own. Get inside, lock up, and I'll go. But not until you're safely home."

"Why do you care?" I asked bitterly, hugging my arms tighter to my middle.

His eyes flashed as he fixed me with an intense stare, pinpoints of light glittering over the dark pools. The effect was mesmerizing, and for a moment, everything fell away except for the two of us. "You're innocent," he rumbled. "I don't hurt innocent women. And I don't let them get hurt. Especially when they're as reckless as you are. There are other monsters lurking in the dark."

That final remark needled at me, and I broke away from his deep gaze. "Yes, you've said that," I managed to scoff. "Funny how you're the only one I've ever seen."

He jerked back as though I'd slapped him. "Fair

enough," he said tightly. "Doesn't change anything. I'm not going anywhere until you're safely in your apartment."

I shifted on the bench, confusion tangling my thoughts. I should be terrified that my captor was standing over me, but he was acting as though he was my protector. I didn't know what to do with that, so I sat stiffly for several more seconds, silently willing him to leave me alone.

As though that would work. The man was a stubborn monster, I'd give him that.

"Fine," I bit out. "I'm going home now. Happy?" I pushed to my feet and immediately swayed, my shaky body wobbling on my high heels.

A strong arm closed around me, long fingers bracketing my waist to support my weight. I tried to jerk away, but I only managed to stumble. Max made a rumbling sound of unmistakable disapproval, and my spine went rigid with indignation. He didn't let me go.

"Those things are a death trap." He scowled at my designer shoes. "I'm walking you to your door. Don't bother arguing. You can't walk straight, and I don't feel like scooping you up out of the way of oncoming traffic again." When I still didn't take a step forward, he sighed. "Are you going to walk, or am I going to have to carry you? Your choice."

"I'm walking," I said through gritted teeth. "You're infuriating as well as insane, you know that?"

He kept his arm braced around me as we started to cross the street. "Yeah, and so are you."

I huffed out a furious breath, but he held me as firmly as ever. The man clearly wasn't even a tiny bit intimidated by me or my considerable anger. With his huge, muscular frame folded around mine to protect me from falling, I couldn't deny that I truly wasn't a threat to him. The very idea was laughable.

We reached my door, and I fumbled in my purse until my fingers found my keys. "You can go now," I said as coolly as I could manage. I didn't want to open my door when he was so close. The memory of his body pinning mine to the wall as he drugged me was still horrifically clear in my mind. A residual shudder of revulsion rolled through me.

He finally released me, stepping away quickly as though I'd become white-hot. "I said I wouldn't hurt you, and I meant it," he rumbled. "Now that I believe you won't go tattling on me to your father, I'll leave you alone."

I stiffened. *Tattling?* That made it sound as though my abduction and interrogation had been child's play. I pressed my lips together, locking my retort inside.

"I'm home. You can leave," I reiterated, giving him a pointed stare.

His chin lifted, and he stared right back at me with those dark eyes. "I'm not leaving until that door locks behind you. If you want me to go, hurry up and do it."

A sound like a growl that I'd never made before slipped between my teeth, and I jammed my key into the lock with more force than necessary. I quickly slipped inside and slammed the door in his scarred face, turning the deadbolt behind me. I pressed my back to the wood and heaved in a deep breath.

I waited until I heard his heavy boots stomping away, fading into the night as he finally left me alone. A tremor wracked my body, and I slid to the floor as all the strength drained out of me. I huddled there for a long time, my bleeding knees stinging and my heart racing.

Max Ferrara had saved my life. He'd grabbed me out of the street before that car could hit me, and he'd gently checked my injuries. He'd insisted on walking me home and seeing me safely inside.

And he still wanted to punish my father for some imaginary sin. Max had sworn that he would leave me alone, but I didn't think for one second that he was out of my life for good.

CHAPTER 7

*T*he blood on my hands irritated me. Usually, I didn't even notice the hot, thick slide down my fingers while I went to work with my knife. But now…

Mere hours ago, I'd been touching Alexandra with these hands. She'd been shockingly soft and feminine in a way I'd forced myself to forget. It'd been two years since I'd touched any woman, and in that time, my world had been coated in blood.

Alexandra was innocent, completely removed from this ugly, violent world. She'd been so delicate and warm in my arms, clinging to me for protection.

My stomach soured, and my mouth twisted in a grimace. The man tied to the chair before me whimpered at the horror of my fearsome expression, but my scowl wasn't directed at him.

Protection. The thought was ridiculous. I was no one's protector, especially not Ron Fitzgerald's daughter.

When that stupid high heel had turned her ankle, I'd acted on instinct to pull her out of the way of traffic. It was the least I could do, since I'd terrorized her in my basement. She was entirely oblivious to her father's corruption, but I couldn't take back what I'd done to her.

Blood seeped into my shirt as I rubbed against the strange ache at the center of my chest. Holding her had felt good. Having her hold on to me had felt good.

Pathetic. Acid coated my tongue. The only reason she hadn't recoiled from me was because she'd been shaken up from almost getting run over.

I should've left her alone as soon as I pulled her to safety. But I'd stayed with her. I'd checked her for injuries. I'd insisted on walking her to her door, like we were on some kind of goddamn date and I was a fucking gentleman.

I released a frustrated growl, and the man tied to the chair cowered.

"Please," he begged. "I have children."

I rolled my eyes, impatient to get past the point of lies. "No, you don't. I picked you because no one will really miss you. Will they, Kirill?"

My blade glinted in the spare light of the single bulb overhead, and he screamed.

Alexandra had been tied to this same chair not very long ago. She'd screamed, too.

The ache in my chest intensified, and I grimaced. I'd made sure not to hurt her. My ruined face alone had been enough to make her weep.

But she hadn't wept when I'd saved her from getting hit by that car. She hadn't been particularly grateful, either. She'd huffed at me and warned me to stop my vendetta against her father.

As though that would ever happen.

Questioning her had gotten me nowhere. I'd frightened an innocent woman, and the memory of her tear-streaked face made my stomach turn.

Taking her had been a terrible mistake. She didn't deserve my retribution. But scum like Kirill did.

The man trafficked heroin for the Bratva. He was one of the most important men I'd ever dared to grab, but I was getting desperate. I couldn't risk drawing the full ire of the Russians, not when my family was so vulnerable—half of us were still imprisoned. But if Kirill talked, it would be worth it.

"You know something about your boss' ties to Ron Fitzgerald." I said it like a condemnation, a known fact. "Tell me."

The whites of his eyes were huge, his brown irises thin rings around dilated pupils. He licked his bloody lips. "Mr. Ivanov's relationship with Fitzgerald is purely political. That's all I know. It's exactly what it looks like."

Yes, it was public knowledge that Mikhail Ivanov, billionaire businessman, was an ardent supporter of Ron Fitzgerald's politics. What the public didn't know was that Ivanov controlled the Bratva in New York, and Fitzgerald knew all about it.

I bared my teeth and leaned in close, allowing him to get a good look at my horrific face. The scar was an indelible mark of my deepest shame, but I'd also learned to use it to my benefit. I'd been tempered by agony, but I'd survived. Now, my outer appearance mirrored the monstrous things I was capable of. I would do whatever it took to restore my family to their rightful place. To restore my own honor.

Kirill cringed, but there was nowhere for him to go. He would never leave this basement alive. How much pain he endured was up to him.

The memory of Alexandra's suffering might shred me like a knife, but I was coolly detached from Kirill's agonized pleas. He wasn't quite human, so hurting him meant nothing to me.

I shifted my knife so that it gleamed before his

eyes, allowing him to see the drops of his own blood that I'd already drawn—a warning that I would take more if he didn't answer my questions.

"I want proof," I hissed. "Evidence that Fitzgerald is corrupt. You're going to tell me where I can find some, or I'll make this last a whole lot longer."

"Wait, wait!" He swallowed hard, and his eyes darted around the room as though to check he wouldn't be overheard. "I don't have any evidence, but Kelvin McCrae does. He bragged to me about it one time when we were gambling in one of his buildings. Everyone knows how McCrae likes to brag."

The man was babbling, but I leaned back and nodded for him to continue. My posture was expectant, casual. But I scarcely dared to breathe in case I missed a single nuance of this confession.

Kelvin McCrae was one of the richest men in the country, and he was a close personal friend to Fitzgerald. McCrae had a reputation for being a *big personality*, which was rich-people speak for *obnoxious asshole*. He wanted everyone to acknowledge that he was a clever businessman, and he desperately wanted prestige.

When Kirill said that McCrae had bragged to him, I believed it. The billionaire real estate developer was known for making shady sales to foreign investors. Like shady Russian *businessman* Kirill here. McCrae wasn't Ivanov, but I knew that the man had strong ties to the Bratva, just like Fitzgerald.

"What did McCrae tell you?" I demanded when Kirill stalled out on a desperate sob. The scent of urine soured the dank air.

"H-he bragged that he's more powerful than the mayor. He has insurance in case Fitzgerald ever turns on him. He said something about the circumstances of his wife's death."

"She died in a fire," I prompted, impatient for him to gasp less and talk more. Everyone knew that Marie Fitzgerald had tragically died in a house fire ten years ago. It was part of Ron Fitzgerald's story of personal loss and resilience.

Kirill shook his head vigorously. "It sounded like more than that. Whatever it was, McCrae helped Fitzgerald cover it up. He kept the receipts, just in case."

My heart hammered against my ribcage. This was the closest I'd ever gotten to real proof of the beloved mayor's corruption.

I pressed my knife to Kirill's throat. My hand shook slightly from a rush of anticipation, and the blade nicked the delicate skin by his artery.

"What kind of receipts? What did they cover up?"

The Russian's body convulsed on a sob. "I-I don't

know! McCrae said something about pulling the original reports. Maybe the results of the arson investigation? I don't know!" he cried when I increased the pressure of my knife. "He just said he used his money and connections to make the whole thing go away as a personal favor to Fitzgerald, but he kept the original records for himself."

I paused, scowling down at Kirill. He'd officially outlived his usefulness. I had a much more important target now.

Kelvin McCrae was one of the most influential men in New York. Getting to him would be my biggest challenge yet. Bigger even than kidnapping and interrogating Alexandra.

Something teased at the back of my mind. If what Kirill was saying was true, Alexandra's mother had died under suspicious circumstances ten years ago, not simply in an accidental house fire.

My own family had been sent to prison ten years ago. The fire had famously happened around the same time; Ron Fitzgerald had nearly lost everything just as he was achieving his greatest victory: taking down the Mafia.

I'd never really thought about my enemy's loss before. But now...

Alexandra's wide, gemstone green eyes glittered across my thoughts. I had a terrible suspicion about what'd really happened to her mother. If I was right, she would definitely recoil from me in true horror.

The memory of our final moments together played through my mind, needling me with sharp, hot pinpricks of shame. She'd reluctantly allowed me to hold her while I walked her to her door; she'd been too irritated with me to remember to be afraid. But once we'd neared her personal sanctuary, she'd shuddered and cringed away from me.

She'd come to her senses and recalled what I really was: a monster in the dark.

She would never let me close enough to touch her again.

I shook my head sharply. I didn't have a reason to touch her. Alexandra wasn't going to report me to the authorities. My business with her was done. There was no reason for me to ever see her again. No matter how much I might want to.

CHAPTER 8

"*A*re you feeling okay, sweetheart? You look tired." My father's warm hazel eyes were soft with concern, but his mouth pressed in a thin, disapproving line.

"I'm fine!" I said, too quickly. I didn't want him to think I was hungover, but telling him the real reason for the dark circles under my eyes was out of the question. No way could I risk revealing that Max Ferrara had been stalking me, and I'd spent a sleepless night haunted by the terrible, itching sensation that I was still being watched.

Nervously, I plucked at the cloth napkin in my lap to divert my anxious energy. If I shifted in my seat beneath the weight of his scrutiny, I wouldn't have a hope of resisting his command for me to return to the safety of my childhood home.

Just as I feared, his brow wrinkled, and his chin took on the tilt of paternal seriousness that meant he was about to try to strongarm me into something I didn't want to do. "Did you go out again last night, Allie?"

I didn't dare lie. I was a terrible liar, and he'd know immediately if I completely fabricated something. Hedging the truth was my best shot at getting out of this. If he continued this line of questioning, he would demand that I come home where he could keep a protective eye on me.

I'd almost suffocated under the weight of his concern for my entire life. My dad loved me, but I couldn't go back to that house. He would smother me, and I loved him too much to allow that old resentment to continue festering between us.

"Yes," I admitted, my cheeks flaming despite my best efforts not to appear guilty. I hadn't done anything wrong, but Daddy already thought I'd gone into work hungover yesterday. My only option now was to dig myself deeper into that hole and hope for the best. "I went out with Isabel, Davis, and Charlie. But it's the weekend," I said quickly. "I worked really hard at the office, and I was stressed by the end of the day. I needed to see my friends and relax a little. I'm twenty-one, Daddy," I reminded him, barely managing to straighten my spine. "I can go out on a Friday night if I want to."

His heavy sigh weighed on my shoulders like a ton of lead, and I shrank into my seat despite my best efforts. "I keep forgetting that you're a young woman now," he admitted. "It's hard for me to see you struggling like this."

My heart squeezed. It would almost be easier if he railed at me for being a failure. This fatherly concern made something crumble in my chest.

He rested an elbow on the table and propped his chin on his hand as he leaned toward me, our beautiful pancake brunch forgotten. In that moment, it was just my dad and me; the buzz of other late morning diners faded into the background, and my full focus centered on him as I waited for more of his censure. I barely breathed as the awful anticipation crushed my lungs, iron bands winding tighter around my chest with each passing second.

"I wish your mother were here." His eyes began to shine, and a lump instantly formed in my throat. "She would know what to say. I know I've never been good at some of this parenting stuff. But I want to be here for you, Allie."

"You are," I said quickly, forcing the vehement words through my constricted airway. "You've always been here for me."

He swallowed hard and managed a tight nod.

Oh, god. Daddy rarely talked about Mom, and when he did, it shredded both of us. Even though a decade had passed since the awful night when we'd lost her, he still loved her as keenly as ever. Our love for her and our loss cut like a knife, inflicting a permanent wound that would never fully heal.

The fire had claimed everything that night: our home, my mother, my childhood. Nothing had been right since the day she'd died. We'd both failed to save her as our house burned, the consuming flames taking her life along with everything else.

My screams still seemed to burn my throat, and the iron bands around my chest were the phantom weight of my father's arms, restraining me from running back into the fire to save her.

"I miss her too," I managed hoarsely, reaching out to clasp my dad's hand. His fingers closed around mine, and he briefly squeezed his eyes shut. "I love you, Daddy."

His grip tightened in a pulse of warm comfort. "I love you too." He scrubbed at his red-rimmed eyes with his free hand and drew in a shuddering breath. "Sorry, princess. I didn't mean to get emotional. Eat your pancakes." He released my hand and tilted his head at my untouched meal.

Dutifully, I took a bite. The syrupy sweetness was

cloying on my ashen tongue, but I managed to force myself to swallow. If I just acted normal, Daddy wouldn't be so sad. I couldn't stand to see him hurting. For so many years, he'd done everything he could to protect me, and in turn, I'd protected him by concealing the worst of my suffering. I couldn't bear to add to his constant pain over the loss of my mother. So, I'd endured the bullying in silence. If he knew about it—if he knew that Gavin was still messing with me—he would definitely drag me back home and keep me close to ensure my safety and happiness.

He'd never been able to understand that I couldn't be happy when I didn't have any freedom. Going to college and meeting my friends had been the best thing that'd ever happened to me, and it was a minor miracle that he'd allowed me to move out on my own this summer.

I forced down another bite of my pancakes, proving that I was okay. Even if it was almost painful to choke down the food.

I managed a small smile and changed the subject, my voice an octave too high as I attempted a breezy tone. "Mr. Callahan and I had a good talk yesterday. You gave me great advice." The muscles around my mouth stretched into a strained grin. "I took responsibility for being late, and he was totally understanding. He actually praised me for my work ethic. It went way better than I ever could've hoped."

Dad returned my smile, the corners of his lips twitching with the effort. "Mike's a great guy. I'm glad that you're on good terms. I know how hard you work, sweetheart. I don't say it enough, but I'm proud of you."

The lump in my throat swelled, and my eyes burned. Daddy never told me he was proud of me. Well, I could count the times he'd said it on one hand. I modeled my life choices in pursuit of making him proud; my father was a great man, and his pride meant everything to me.

"Thanks, Daddy." My voice hitched on his name, and I quickly swiped at my eyes.

He let out a watery laugh and raked a hand through his silver-tinged copper hair, leaving the neat style uncharacteristically mussed. "Sorry, I didn't mean for this brunch to be so emotional. Why don't you tell me about your internship. Are you working on any good cases?"

I leapt on the change of subject, eager to talk about something normal and safe. "Well, you know I'm mostly copying files and carrying coffee, but it's amazing being in the office, surrounded by all those brilliant legal minds. I'm so happy that I got my placement. I really hope I can work there after law school."

His smile broadened with genuine delight. "I'm sure you will, sweetheart."

"But I don't want you to pull any strings," I hastened to add. "I'm going to get there on my own merit."

"I know that too." His grin turned a bit wry. "You've always been so stubborn about being independent."

I nodded, letting that stinging comment roll off my back. He didn't realize it stung. I might've been advocating for my independence for my entire life, but he'd barely allowed me any personal freedoms. Before college, leaving the house to socialize without a chaperone of his choosing had been out of the question. Not that I had many invitations to socialize. But sometimes I wondered if I would've been less of a freak if I'd been allowed to integrate with my peers a bit more.

"You okay, princess?"

Damn it, I hadn't managed to keep my expression pleasantly neutral. All this stuff with Max and the sleepless nights were chipping away at my usual composure.

Max. He thought Daddy was involved in some sort of conspiracy with the Bratva. If I could only prove to him that it wasn't true, then he'd leave my dad alone. His family was guilty, and the Bratva had nothing to do with that fact. Neither did my father.

Who better to ask for details about the Ferrara case than the man who'd brought them down?

"Yeah," I replied. "I'm okay. I, um, part of why I've been so exhausted is because I'm trying to learn more about the Five Families case."

His brows rose. "You've been studying my Mafia case? Why?"

"Well, Mr. Callahan was involved, wasn't he? You know I cited his work on the Kassel case in my law school admissions essay. I was thinking about expanding my study of his career."

Daddy gave me an affected frown, but his eyes danced with a teasing light. "You're more impressed with Mike Callahan than your old man?"

I ducked my head, my cheeks heating from the lies I was spinning while staying as close to the truth as possible. "I don't want to go into politics. You know that. I'd rather stay in Law. Mr. Callahan has had a long and successful career at the U.S. Attorney's Office."

"I'm just giving you a hard time," he assured me with a soft smile. "I don't want you to go into politics, either. It's not a life I would want for you."

I nodded again, not questioning the familiar

statement. Daddy had never pressured me to follow in his footsteps. He was pleased with my choice to pursue Law, but he'd been candid that politics wasn't always pleasant. Above all, he wanted to protect me from any potential pain or suffering.

What he wanted wasn't reality, but in this aspect, he didn't have to worry. I'd much rather work pro bono cases and barely scrape by than be a famous, beloved politician like my dad.

And I had plenty of time to work as a lawyer and save up before switching primarily to pro bono. Daddy might even help support me once I made the change. He remembered how passionate Mom had been about helping abused women find stability and empowerment. He would definitely approve of my choice to pursue prosecution to get justice for victimized women.

Max's dark eyes flashed across my mind. *I don't hurt innocent women.*

He'd told me he was a monster, but he'd been careful not to hurt me while he was interrogating me. Then, he'd saved my life last night.

I remembered the gentleness of his thick fingers on my legs as he'd checked me for injuries. My skin still tingled at the thought of those big hands wrapped around my calves, holding me with aching care.

Max wasn't pure evil. Not like the men who abused the women I'd helped while volunteering at the shelter. He didn't find sadistic pleasure in scaring me. Kidnapping me had been a desperate means to an end: seeing through his deranged vendetta against my dad.

I had to reason with him. If I just understood his family's crimes better, I could prove to him that the Bratva had nothing to do with the case that had sent them to prison. Even if the Russians were tangentially involved, that didn't absolve his family. All Daddy had done was bring them to justice. If I could make Max see that, I could protect my father from his misguided retribution.

"So, what about the Mafia case?" I prompted, keeping my dad focused on what I needed to know. "Who were the five crime families you took down, again? Gambino, Lucchese, and Ferrara, right?"

"That's right. And the Colombo and Maranzano crime families. I'm not surprised if you don't remember the details. You were only eleven when we won that case, and I tried to keep work life and home life separate."

"Do you think I could access the old case files?" I pressed. Usually, I never wanted him to pull strings for me, but to protect him from Max's vengeance, I would allow it. "Maybe Mr. Callahan could point me in the right direction."

"You seem to have a good relationship with Mike already," he approved. "I'm sure he'll give you access to anything you want to look at. Especially if it's to further your career aspirations. It sounds like he values your work, and if he's smart, he'll want to hire you as soon as your get your Law degree. If he throws up any roadblocks, let me know, and I'll make a call."

For once, I didn't vehemently refuse his offer of assistance. "Thanks, Daddy."

I would get evidence of the Ferrara family's crimes, no matter what it took. Then, I could show Max the cold hard proof that his family deserved to be sent to jail and prove that my dad hadn't been working with the Bratva.

I didn't allow myself to worry about how my mercurial captor would react to the news, but anything was better than him hurting my dad. Max would see reason. I wouldn't accept any other outcome.

CHAPTER 9

ALLIE

*I*t took over a week of sleepless nights and multiple meetings with Mike before I compiled enough evidence to show Max. The photos and personal accounts in the case files were often violent enough to turn my stomach, and once I'd even gotten sick after opening a file to photos from a murder scene.

More like execution. Max's uncle, Tony Ferrara, had been responsible for that particularly vicious crime. He was still serving out his sentence in prison and would be for another eight years, at least. Max's father and grandfather, on the other hand, were both walking free now. His grandfather, Michael, had been convicted of fraud. And his father, Paul, had been convicted of drug trafficking and racketeering.

They'd only gotten out of prison two years ago, early releases for good behavior.

I'd still barely scratched the surface of the mountain of evidence the U.S. Attorney's Office had gathered against the Five Families, but I'd narrowed my focus to the Ferraras. I had plenty of proof to show Max.

Now, I just had to find him. Even though it should've been a relief that I hadn't glimpsed him in the shadows since the night I'd confronted him in the street, his absence didn't lessen the nightmares that haunted me in the few hours I did manage to sleep. Several times, I'd dreamt of falling, my knees cracking against the pavement, a blaring car horn, and strong arms around me. I awoke from those with my brow damp and my heart racing. The jittery sensation was scarcely better than the visions of bloody corpses and the tear-streaked faces of bereaved family members left behind.

I ran a shaky hand through my hair and resisted the urge to rub my dry eyes, which were itchy from sleep deprivation. I didn't want to risk smudging the concealer I'd applied to hide the worst of my dark circles. I knew I must look like a frazzled mess, just like I'd felt on the inside ever since Max had first abducted me.

There had only been one way for me to narrow

down his location. His father's address was on file with the authorities, and I had access to those records. He might've been released from federal prison early, but he was still on probation.

My knees shook slightly as I approached the historic townhouse in the heart of Manhattan's Upper East Side. Apparently, Paul Ferrara had lost several years of his freedom but not his lavish home when he'd been arrested. I was about to knock on a notorious mobster's door.

Maybe Max was right; maybe I had gone insane.

I took a deep breath, reminding myself that my father's safety was on the line, and Paul Ferrara hadn't been convicted of any violent crimes. Of course, I wasn't stupid enough to think he hadn't been aware of some of those crimes when they took place, but I didn't have to fear for my immediate safety.

I hoped.

Summoning my resolve to protect my family, I lifted a trembling finger and punched the doorbell before I could think better of it.

After several agonizing minutes, the door opened, and a stunning woman greeted me with a cool expression and even colder black eyes. Her delicate chin lifted, and even though she was an inch shorter than me, her imperious stare made me feel tiny and weak in her petite shadow.

"Yes?" she prompted, sounding almost bored.

"Hi," I breathed, barely managing to prevent myself from stuttering. This woman definitely gave off ruthless-Mafia vibes, and it was all I could do to keep my spine straight beneath her withering glare. "I'm here to see Max?" I silently cursed myself when what was meant to be a confident statement came out as a lilting question.

Dark, perfectly arched brows rose almost all the way to her sleek black hair, which was pulled back from her heart-shaped face. Her aloof beauty was almost painfully intimidating. My stomach twisted, and for a moment, I considered bolting.

"And who are you?" she demanded, her voice soft and slightly husky. Everything about her oozed poise and cool confidence. I felt terribly disheveled and pathetically weak in comparison, my composure completely shot after so many sleepless nights. The relentless fear for my father that'd followed me every waking minute had left me shredded and raw.

"Allie." I almost squeaked my name, but I pressed on. I was here now. I had to follow through. "I've, ah, been out with Max a few times."

Those brows lifted higher. "And he gave you this address?"

"Yes?" Damn it. I'd asked a question again when it should've been a calm statement.

I am strong. I am independent. I can do this.

I squared my shoulders, toughening my resolve. "I can come back later if he's not here."

Tell me where I can find him. I silently willed her to reveal his location. The sooner I could leave this place, the better.

Her eyes scanned me once again, picking apart each of my features with cold precision. Her sudden, broad smile was jarringly beautiful. The icy woman had been replaced by a dazzling hostess in the blink of an eye. Despite her suddenly welcoming demeanor, I was more unnerved than ever.

"He must not have wanted to show you his shit-hole apartment," she said, the snide comment tinkling on a little laugh. "This is a much more impressive address. Why didn't you let him know you were coming?"

I didn't miss the incisive flash of her obsidian eyes as she interrogated me. The woman was a shark, even if she was hiding her razor-sharp teeth.

"I broke my phone and lost all my contacts." It was the smoothest lie I'd ever told. This woman could flay me with a single glance, and I had no choice but to pull on my thickest emotional armor. It was pure survival instinct, tempered by years of terrible bullying. I never thought I'd be grateful for the hard lessons those years had taught me, but they would possibly save my skin now.

Her brow furrowed, all sympathy and understanding. "Oh, that's the worst. Why don't you come in? I'll call him for you."

"That's okay," I said quickly, shifting back an inch before I could stop myself. "If you wouldn't mind giving me his number, I can contact him."

"Don't be silly." She waved away my request, that beatific smile still glowing like a warning beacon. "If you're dating my little brother, I'd love to get to know you. We can chat while we wait for him to come home."

I swallowed hard. This terrifying woman was Max's sister? Now that she'd mentioned it, I could see the resemblance, especially in the eyes and around her full mouth. Only where Max's eyes burned with rage, hers glinted with cold calculation.

"Come in," she urged when I hesitated. "I'll call him now. I'm sure he'll get here quickly."

I definitely didn't like the little twist to her lush lips when she spoke. Why would she think Max would rush home to see me? Did she suspect that I was a threat to their family somehow? Had she been in on Max's scheme to abduct and interrogate me in the first place?

"He hasn't dated anyone since the accident," she supplied, pretending she didn't register my reluctance as she stepped aside in an attempt to usher me through the front door.

I barely stopped myself from clutching my locket as anxiety gripped my body like a vise. She wasn't offering to share his number, and I didn't know how I would track him down otherwise.

I took a moment to process what she'd said. It made sense that she'd be wary of any woman who might date her brother, especially if he truly hadn't been with anyone since his face had been scarred. I had no idea when the injury had been inflicted, but girlfriends showing up to his house must be out of the ordinary.

She'd also mentioned a *shithole apartment,* which meant Max didn't live here with his family, despite the fact that the house was massive. Of course my presence here would seem weird. I'd shown up out of the blue and asked for Max at the wrong address.

Still, it would be beyond stupid for me to walk into that house. The memory of what'd happened the last time I was alone with a Ferrara in a private space was all too clear in my mind: I'd been tied to a chair in a basement and questioned by a madman.

This house probably had a basement too.

"If you don't mind calling him, I'd appreciate it."

My voice barely wavered. I could excuse that as nerves at meeting my supposed boyfriend's sister. "I can wait out here. I don't want to impose."

"Don't be silly." Her brilliant grin practically dazzled me, but her predatory eyes kept my feet firmly rooted on the concrete step.

She blew out a sigh and closed the door behind her, joining me outside. "I'll call him. I get that it can be intimidating to meet the family of the person you're dating. Especially if it's a new relationship." She was all smiles and understanding as she pulled her phone out of her pocket and found Max's contact details.

She connected the call, and to my surprise, she put it on speaker. The four rings that sounded as we waited for Max to pick up seemed to clang through my system like alarm bells, setting my body on high alert.

"He doesn't like to take my calls." She confided in me like we were sharing a sad secret. "He's been different since the accident. Private, you know?"

I swallowed and managed a silent nod. My fine hairs stood on end, and every instinct was screaming at me to get the hell away from this woman and her false social niceties.

"What, Francesca?" Max's voice cracked through the air like a thunderclap, and I jolted.

"Someone's here to see you." Her voice took on a slightly singsong lilt. "Come to the house."

"Who?" he barked. That harsh, impatient tone was all too familiar to me by now. I heard it in my nightmares.

She glanced at me. "What did you say your name was, hon? Allie?"

A beat of silence, then a harsh curse.

Francesca let out another melodic laugh. "Don't you want to see your new girlfriend?" That lilt took on a taunting edge. "She looks like she's too good for you anyway." She fixed me with an affected pout. "She wouldn't even come into the house to wait for you. What have you been telling her about your family, little brother? We're perfectly hospitable."

"She's not my girlfriend," he growled.

Francesca's eyes glinted cruelly. "That's too bad. She's very pretty. You might think you're too ugly for her, but she did come here to see you."

I stiffened at the underhanded comment about his disfigurement. She'd said that Max hadn't dated since *the accident.* It implied that the injury had occurred after he was old enough to be interested in dating. I'd been up close and personal with that devastatingly handsome face that'd been marred by the horrific scar. Max must've been breathtaking before he'd been injured so severely. I suspected that

Francesca's cruel words landed a harsh blow to a deep emotional wound.

"Tell her I'll see her later." Max's grim words seemed to be spoken through gritted teeth.

"But she said she broke her phone and lost your number." Francesca spoke with the weight of a tragedy. "Isn't that right, Allie?"

"Yes." I flung the word at her in a bold challenge, a reflexive response to a bully. Francesca might have a gorgeous smile, but she was clearly a master at cutting a person down to nothing with her sharp, conniving insults.

I raised my voice slightly and addressed Max. "I need to see you, Max."

A wordless growl. He was pissed.

My stomach did a funny flip, but I kept my shoulders back and allowed my stare to clash with Francesca's. I'd risked everything to come here and give Max the evidence that would save my father. I wouldn't back down now, especially not because of this bully.

"Did you hear that?" she practically cooed. "Allie *needs you*, Max. She's very sweet, isn't she? How did you ever convince her to go out with a monster like you?"

I glowered at her, no longer caring that she was the daughter of an infamous criminal or that I was standing outside Paul Ferrara's house. Based on her taunts, it seemed that she didn't know who I was; she hadn't been in on the whole kidnapping-and-interrogation thing.

Indignant anger brought out my reckless streak. "I'm waiting right here." I said it as a challenge to her and as a demand to Max. "I'll see you soon, Max."

"I'm on my way."

Francesca ended the call with a snide smile. "A little overly eager, aren't we? Take my advice. Desperation isn't a good look, Allie. Especially when you're chasing after roadkill like my brother."

My rage swelled, and my fingers clenched to fists at my sides. *Oh, you bitch.* I knew her kind, but the fact that she could be so cruel to her own family was beyond disgusting.

"It's not Max's fault if he was in an accident," I asserted. "Why should I hold that against him?"

She cocked her head at me, her pillowy lips taking on a nasty twist, as though she relished the flavor of her next taunt. "How do you know it wasn't his fault? Didn't he tell you what happened?"

I stiffened. Of course, Max hadn't told me how he'd been scarred. He hadn't told me anything about himself at all except for the fact that he hated my father. And that he protected innocent women.

He might be insane, but he'd saved my life. And it

seemed I'd been right to think that he'd suffered ridicule and rejection because of his disfigurement. He'd been bullied, too. And by his own family, no less. That was enough to earn my defensiveness on his behalf.

I lifted my chin and stared Francesca down. "He didn't have to tell me what happened for me to know that he didn't deserve to be hurt like that. No one does."

Her smile sharpened, a baring of those shark's teeth. "Are you sure? You seem very naïve, hon. Do yourself a favor and get the hell away from my brother. It won't end well for you."

A threat? From this bitch?

Nope.

I'd dealt with a monster holding me captive in a dark basement. I could handle a vindictive woman in broad daylight. She thought she could scare off her brother's first supposed girlfriend since his accident had left him permanently scarred?

No way. It didn't matter that I wasn't really his girlfriend. It didn't matter that Max's twisted snarl still haunted my dreams. All that mattered was that this bitch was tormenting her brother, a man who'd already suffered through so much pain that it'd driven him to madness.

The same man who'd pulled me out of the deadly

path of an oncoming car and then insisted on seeing me safely to my door. Yes, Max had terrorized me, but he'd also saved me. He was mercurial and deeply conflicted, but he wasn't pure evil. When I'd been tied up in that basement, I'd recognized his pain. It was what had driven him to kidnap and question me. Even on that awful night, he hadn't laid a hand on me.

Max wasn't violent or innately cruel, but his sister clearly relished engaging in psychological warfare.

I returned her imperious stare and icy demeanor. "You don't have to wait out here with me. I'm sure Max will be here soon."

Her nasty little smile stayed in place. "Yes, I'm sure he'll rush home. He won't want me to scare you off."

"I'm not scared."

Another tinkling laugh. "I knew you were too good for my brother."

I crossed my arms over my chest and pressed my lips together, not deigning to reply. If she wanted to stand out here and needle me with insults about Max, that was her prerogative. I didn't have to continue to engage.

She leaned a shoulder against the front door, making an ostentatious show of settling in to wait.

Fine. We could stare at each other in stony silence.

You don't scare me, bully.

Her beautiful face remained mildly amused, immune to my glower. I didn't bother mirroring her nonchalance. I didn't hide behind false smiles. I met bullies head-on. Strength was the language they understood best.

After an interminable period of time, Max's harsh voice punched through the silent tension that'd built between his sister and me. "Jesus, Bambi."

His long fingers wrapped around my wrist, and my skin tingled where his callouses brushed against my highly sensitized nerves; I'd been on full alert while sparring with Francesca, and his sudden grip shattered my outwardly thorny demeanor.

"Max!" I released his name on a gasp, stumbling after him as he yanked me away from his sister. He pulled me close to his side and tucked me beneath his strong arm. I wasn't sure if he was shielding me from her or if he was simply intent on dragging me somewhere to berate me privately.

"Let's go," he rumbled, pulling me along as he strode away from his family home.

"It was lovely to meet you, Allie!" Francesca called after me, that singsong lilt ending in a delighted giggle.

I stopped resisting Max's strength and did my best to match his long strides, grateful to get away from his bitchy sister. Withstanding her cruelty had tapped out the little emotional reserves I had left after suffering through so many sleepless nights. I blew out a heavy sigh and relaxed into Max, allowing him to whisk me somewhere far away from his awful family.

CHAPTER 10

"*W*here are we going?" Her voice was breathy from the exertion of matching my longer strides, and I couldn't help but imagine what it would sound like if she gasped my name.

Over the long nights that'd passed since I'd saved her from getting hit by that car, I'd obsessively thought about our moments together: her flashing eyes, those long legs, her desperate grip on my arms as I checked her for injuries.

Fuck, I hadn't realized the depth of my fixation until I pulled her away from my cruel sister. Now, I was playing out the fantasy again in real time. I had her slight body tucked against my side, carrying her away from danger. Protecting her.

"Somewhere far away from my sister," I bit out,

frustrated with the direction of my thoughts. I should be furious with her for daring to show up at my family home, but instead, I was furious with myself for craving her. "I can't believe you told Francesca you're my girlfriend."

Something hot and possessive burned in my chest, and I pulled her closer. I gritted my teeth and shoved that possessiveness deep down. I had no business feeling possessive of Alexandra Fitzgerald. It was pathetic that I would even react to the idea that she said she was my girlfriend.

I'd spent far too much time obsessing over her, just because she was the first woman I'd touched in years. It was time to cut that shit out. My fixation was bad for us both. Especially since she'd forced her way back into my life. How was I supposed to forget about how soft and delicate she felt in my arms when she gave me no choice but to hold her?

"You really are insane, Bambi," I ground out. "What the hell were you thinking?"

She stiffened, but I continued to hustle her along, driven to put as much space as possible between her and my sister. If Francesca found out who she really was—Fitzgerald's daughter—there would be hell to pay.

I had to get her far away from my family, for both our sakes.

"I need to talk to you," she insisted, as though that wasn't completely crazy. "You think I wanted to go to your father's house? I didn't have a choice."

I glared down at her. "Of course you had a choice. I promised to leave you alone, and now you've decided to come looking for me?" The woman must have a death wish. "How many times do I have to tell you how dangerous I am?"

"Don't bother," she retorted breezily, seemingly oblivious to the fact that she'd just put herself in the crosshairs of a criminal syndicate. "You can say it as many times as you want, but you'll be wasting your breath. I won't let you scare me off when you're a threat to my dad. I came to your house to show you something important."

Her steps faltered, but I refused to stop moving. I had to get her away from my family. They couldn't know who she was or what I'd done to her. If I'd succeeded in getting the information from her that I'd wanted, I would've been celebrated by my family. But I'd failed, and I'd risked us all by pulling Fitzgerald's precious daughter into this. If my father found out the reckless risk I'd taken, I would definitely draw his ire rather than his respect.

"Stop." She tried to sound firm and commanding, but I kept walking. She refused to understand the danger she'd put herself in.

"I said stop, Max."

I jerked to a halt and rounded on her, my frustration sparking into anger. She was just as stubborn and reckless as I was, and it was absolutely infuriating.

"What?" I snapped. "What was so important that you risked your safety to show it to me?"

She lifted her chin, and those gemstone green eyes clashed with mine. I glowered down at her. She swallowed hard, but she didn't drop her defiant posture beneath the weight of my menace.

"Evidence," she replied evenly.

My brows rose. She couldn't possibly mean what I thought she meant. That would be utterly idiotic as well as reckless.

"Evidence," I repeated, the word a cold, flat warning. "You decided to look into your father's ties to the Bratva? You really do have a death wish."

I regretted my actions more than ever. She'd never known anything about her father's corruption. She'd been entirely innocent and removed from the situation. Now, she'd plunged into the conspiracy, and if she kept digging, she wouldn't like what she found.

I didn't want that for her. The truth would hurt her, but not nearly as much as my enemies would hurt her if they felt threatened by her actions. Or my own family.

The thought of her screaming for mercy echoed through my mind, taking on the familiar, grating note of my mother's screams. My fists clenched at my sides, and I tasted blood in my mouth as my gnashing teeth tore my cheek.

She bristled, offended. "No, because my father's ties to the Bratva don't exist. I have the evidence from the casefiles of your family's crimes. There's absolutely nothing in there about Bratva involvement. If I can just show you the truth, then—"

"Are you fucking serious?" I cut her off, furious at her for recklessly endangering herself.

She straightened her spine and met my rage head-on, her peridot eyes sparking with her own anger. She was fierce but so small in my shadow. Did she really not have any idea how fucking breakable she was?

"Yes, I'm serious." She reached into her purse and pulled out a flash drive. "This is the evidence my father brought against your family at trial ten years ago. They might've told you a different version of history, but this is proof. They aren't at all innocent, Max. The Bratva had nothing to do with them being sent to jail."

I snatched the drive from her hand and flung it

down on the pavement. A soft sound of protest left her throat when I crushed it beneath my boot.

"I know my family is guilty," I seethed. "You've wasted your time, and you put yourself at risk for nothing. I don't give a shit about their crimes; don't you get that? I care about the scumbag crap that your father pulled. I care that he's the fucking beloved mayor of New York, when his hands are every bit as bloody as my father's. I'm not naïve like you, Bambi." I spat the insult in a harsh rebuke. Maybe if I was an asshole, she'd let go of this pitying crap and see reason. "I know how the world really works. People aren't good. They aren't kind. You live in a gilded fantasy, and if that's where you want to stay in perfect ignorance, that's fine with me. But stop coming to me with your bullshit. I've warned you about this already."

Her freckled cheeks colored to a deep red flush by the time I finished. To my shock, she stepped toward me and lifted her face to mine, getting right in my personal space.

A low growl left my chest as the heat inside me flared into an inferno. Her lush lips were so close to mine, and her scent infused my senses—sweet and delicate, just like her. All I had to do was lower my face mere inches, and I could capture her mouth. I could tame that sharp tongue. I could hold her close and make her melt, until she didn't have a thought in her pretty head, much less thoughts about defying me.

She let out a little warning growl of her own. "I'm not going to allow you to continue this insane vendetta against my father. If you think for one second that I'll leave him vulnerable to your threats, then you're the naïve one. And stop calling me Bambi."

Her chest rose and fell on rapid breaths, and tantalizing images of her panting beneath me filled my mind. I could make her gasp. I could make her beg.

I could make her forget all about everything but me, and she wouldn't think to put herself in danger as long as I had her in my arms.

I came to my senses and snapped my scowl back into place. That fantasy had become far too familiar and far too tempting. There was no way beautiful, innocent Alexandra would ever welcome me into her bed. I was deluding and distracting myself from what was really important: keeping her safe.

I'd been the one to pull her into this mess, and it was on me to protect her, no matter how ludicrous that concept was. Even if that meant protecting her from herself.

She was doing all of this out of loyalty to her

father. She wanted to convince me to drop my vendetta against him because she believed I would hurt him.

I respected her for that loyalty. And I recognized the fierce determination that came along with it. She wouldn't drop this until she felt that her father was safe from harm.

I would have to risk honesty.

"Since you don't seem to care about your own safety, I'll level with you. I'm not going to attack your father." My reluctant admission was so rough that the words sounded like I forced them through a mouthful of barbed wire. "I want leverage against him. I want him to know that I have evidence of what he really is, and that I won't hesitate to use it against him if he ever tries to come after my family again. That's why I questioned you in the first place. I thought you could give me testimony that I could hold over his head. I was never going to hurt you. And I only threatened your father to keep you from going to the cops.

"If I'd known I would have to be your damn babysitter, I never would've approached you in the first place." I raked a hand through my hair, frustrated.

I expected her to recoil at my last remark,

incensed at the insult. Instead, her expression softened.

"Does your family know about what you're doing?" she asked, her tone dropping to a gentler cadence. "Do they know that you're going after my dad?"

When her gaze flicked to the ruined flesh around my eye, I realized that I'd forgotten to hide the worst of the damage to my face. I quickly mussed my hair so that it fell over my brow once again. I'd already shown far too much vulnerability around her. She was hammering against my defenses with her confounding mixture of soft concern and fierce defiance.

I'd never dealt with anyone like her, and I didn't know how to be around her. She put me off-balance in a way I'd never experienced before.

It only made me want her that much more.

My jaw ticked. I shouldn't want her at all. She was an impossibility.

"They know what your father is guilty of," I rumbled. "They know that he worked with the Russians to destroy us."

She eyed me carefully, as though I was a cornered beast that might snap at her if she pressed me too hard. "Why are you doing this for them? I get that you think you're protecting them, but your sister

135

was so cruel to you. Are you really willing to risk going to jail by continuing this plot against my dad? My father has no reason to investigate your family now. There is no threat. So why are you putting yourself at risk for Francesca? Are you close with your parents? Because if you are, I'm sure they wouldn't want you to jeopardize your freedom."

Her words hit my chest like physical blows, and I rocked back on my heels. "You don't know the first thing about my father. Yeah, my sister is a piece of work, and you got a glimpse at her lovely personality today, thanks to your recklessness. Family is more than hugs and coddling. Sometimes love is hard, but blood is everything." I repeated the harsh promise that'd been drilled into me since birth.

She didn't understand how the world worked, but she did understand familial duty. Her loyalty to her father proved as much.

"What about your mother?" she asked, still confoundingly soft and concerned. "Do you think she would want you to risk yourself for this plot against my dad?"

My fury was doused by the distant memory of my mother's cries for mercy, and my heart was suddenly encased in ice. "I wouldn't know." My voice came out flat and cold. "She's dead. She died when I was thirteen. My dad went to prison around the same time, and Francesca had to serve as my legal guardian for five years. She was barely more than a kid herself. Just because my family is fucked up doesn't change the fact that they're my blood."

Alexandra's delicate features pinched with an expression that turned my stomach. "I'm sorry for your loss."

My scowl deepened, and I lashed out. "I already told you I don't want your pity."

Her eyes glittered with the first hint of tears, and something tugged at the center of my chest. "It's not pity. It's empathy. My mother died when I was eleven."

My defensive cruelty crumbled beneath the weight of my regret. "I know. And I'm sorry."

Her lashes fluttered as she blinked away tears. "Thank you." Her voice hitched, and it tore at something deep inside me.

She didn't question how I knew, but I assumed that she reasoned it away. Her mother's death was public knowledge; the information was readily available to anyone who did even a cursory internet search for Ron Fitzgerald.

"I get why you're so fiercely protective of your father," I said, my tone gentling in the face of her grief. "Keep being naïve, Bambi. You'll be happier that way. Leave all this alone, and I'll leave you alone. And I won't hurt your dad."

Instead of relaxing, she stiffened with renewed indignation. "Stop telling me I'm naïve. I'm not stupid, Max. And I'm not weak. I'm not dropping this until you do."

I crossed my arms over my chest. "I didn't say you're stupid. And I'm starting to get that you're not weak, no matter how delicate you look. But you have to keep your pretty nose out of this. The Bratva is far more dangerous to you than I am, and if you keep digging, they'll eventually take notice."

I would never hurt her, but I knew what those animals could do to an innocent woman. I'd never allow them anywhere near Alexandra.

She scoffed, oblivious to the threat they posed. "You don't get it, do you? There is no Bratva conspiracy. I know my dad. He's a good person."

I pressed my lips together, holding in more argumentative words. Clearly, they would get me nowhere.

"I'm sorry I brought this into your life." I didn't bother repeating that she was naïve. That would only piss her off, and I needed her to listen. "What can I say to make you steer clear of all this? I told you I wouldn't let you get hurt, and if you go digging up dirt on the Russians—or even if my own family finds out about your little investigation—you'll have a target on your back."

She met me squarely in the eye, defiant no matter how I tried to reason with her. "You can't make me drop this. Not until you do. You're the threat here, Max. No one else. My dad isn't safe until I convince you to let this go."

I grimaced. "I already told you I'm not going to attack him. Why are you being so difficult?"

She shook her head. "You think you're protecting your family. I'm protecting mine. I'll do whatever I have to do in order to keep my father safe."

I ignored the flutter of fear in my gut and fixed her with a cool stare. "Are you thinking of going to the cops again, Alexandra?" My tone was as cold as steel, but there was no edge to the threat. I'd already showed my hand, and I didn't have much leverage to keep her in line anymore.

Her calm expression didn't betray even a hint of fear in the face of my menace. Why wasn't she afraid of me? It was unbelievably frustrating that she wasn't at all intimidated into cooperating with my demands. Hardened criminals pissed themselves when I scowled in their direction. Alexandra simply flipped her long, shining hair over her shoulder and looked directly into my ruined face.

"No, I won't go to the cops. Because despite what

you did to me, I don't think you deserve to go to jail. Whatever awful thing happened to you, I believe it's driven you to this madness. Jail won't help you."

Shock punched me, but I kept my face carefully blank. "You really think I'm insane?"

"I think you're troubled," she countered gently. "And I think your family told you lies about my dad. You know what?" Her eyes brightened with sudden understanding. "You can keep looking for proof that my father colluded with the Bratva. As long as you're not planning on hurting him, you can investigate to your heart's content. Because you won't find anything to use against him. But I'm still asking you to drop it, for your own sake. Stalking my dad isn't safe. If you're caught, you will go to jail, and I'll have nothing to do with it."

Something swelled at the center of my chest, and I resisted the urge to rub my sternum. Her concern did something weird to me. I wasn't at all comfortable with the sensation.

I blew out a long sigh. At least she'd agreed to walk away from all this. At least she would be safe.

"Okay. That's fine. You just stay out of it, and I'll do what I have to do."

Her eyes tightened with some emotion I couldn't quite identify, and suddenly her hand closed around mine. I stared at her slender fingers where they clutched at me, utterly baffled and a little unnerved.

She was touching me. Willingly. Urgently.

The heat of her tender touch sent a pulse of insidious warmth into my skin. I couldn't bring myself to pull away.

"You don't have to do this," she said softly. "You have a choice, Max."

Her breathy voice on my name sent a shockwave through my body. I clenched my teeth and tore my hand from her grasp before my weakness for her could overwhelm me.

"Then I've made my choice," I bit out. "Go home, Bambi. We're done."

I turned sharply on my heel, forcibly severing the connection between us. Her soft gasp caressed my skin, winding around me like a clinging vine, threatening to bind me in place.

Fuck, I wanted her. I wanted her more than I'd ever wanted a woman. She was soft and fierce at the same time, a contradiction I found fascinating. I wanted her to release that breathy gasp as I claimed a savage kiss. I craved her surrender, to possess her.

My fists clenched at my sides, and my fingernails bit into my palms as I took my first step, wrenching free from her alluring pull. Somehow, I managed to stalk away from her.

She was my enemy's daughter. I'd kidnapped and terrorized her. I had no business being anywhere near her, much less touching her.

No matter how much I wanted her, I had to leave Alexandra Fitzgerald firmly in my past.

CHAPTER 11

"*C*harlie, you take the selfie. You're tallest." As always, Isabel commanded the space around her; her bright smile and effervescent aura were utterly captivating. We all squished together in a tight group hug as Charlie dutifully accepted Isabel's phone.

"Excuse me." Davis pouted. "I'm a short dude, but I'm still taller than Charlie."

"Not when she's wearing heels." Isabel brushed off his touchy remark.

Davis sighed. "And your legs do look killer in those heels, honey. I wish I could pull them off."

"You totally could." I hugged him more tightly to my side. "Come on, smile before my lips seize up. I've already posed for like a hundred photos with my dad."

I was beyond ready to ditch the *mayor's daughter* public persona and just hang out with my friends. These fundraising events were always difficult for me, but my besties made them actually enjoyable. Once I finished with all the photo ops, we could indulge in the sumptuous atmosphere and copious Champagne. The gilded ballroom and glittering decorations were ridiculously fancy this evening, and it promised to be a great night. Kelvin McCrae, Gavin's dad, had been generous enough to offer space in his most prestigious hotel to support my dad's cause.

Yet another reason why I couldn't get Gavin fired.

I shook the small thought of Gavin from my mind before he could sour my night, and I leaned into the selfie with my friends.

"Oh, because it would be such a tragedy if your radiant smile remained fixed in place." Davis huffed at me, but his mouth stretched in a broad grin.

Charlie snapped a handful of pics before we finally released each other and relaxed into more casual postures.

I turned to Davis, my photo-ready smile melting with concern. "You okay? You seem kind of bummed out tonight."

"Yeah," Isabel agreed, focusing on Davis' sour

mood with intense brown eyes. "It's not like you to be this snarky. What's going on?"

He tugged at his tux, straightening the unique navy jacket. He looked so dapper it almost hurt. The man might be a fashion icon one day if his dancing career took off. His five-foot eight-inch frame was densely packed with lithe muscle, and his anvil-square jaw framed the flat planes of his handsome face.

"I just feel kind of blah," he lamented. "I think I'm about to start my period."

Charlie's darkly penciled brows rose to her platinum blond hair. "You don't get a period."

"A sympathy period, then," he amended. "I must be syncing up with one of you. Allie?" He turned sea green eyes on me. "You've seemed kind of down recently. It's you, isn't it? You're pulling me into your cycle."

Despite the twinge in my stomach, a giggle burst from my chest. "Crap, you noticed that? I thought I was doing a good job looking put together. And sorry, but sympathy periods aren't a thing. You can't blame me; you're not getting out of this so easy. Tell us what's up."

He scoffed. "Why do I have three nosey women for best friends?"

"Because we're awesome," Isabel reminded him. "Now, spill."

He grabbed a glass of Champagne from a passing server and took a long gulp. "Johnny broke things off with me." His usually jovial features fell, and my heart tugged toward my hurt friend. "I know it was just a few dates, but I really thought there was a spark. Or something. I don't know. Romance is stupid."

I wrapped him in another one-armed hug. "Don't say that. You love love." I clinked my own glass to his. "Screw Johnny. His beard was too perfectly groomed, anyway. You can't trust a guy who spends that much time in front of a mirror. You deserve someone who will give you their full attention."

"I won't be screwing him. Ever," Davis said glumly.

"Then we'll find you someone better," Isabel said decisively. "I bet there are a dozen guys at this fundraiser who would love to ask you out."

She gestured with her champagne flute, taking in the hundred or so tuxedo-clad men that filled the ballroom. Glamorous women in colorful gowns shimmered like scores of jewels amongst the sea of black and white.

"I don't know." Davis took another gulp of his

drink. "I don't think I'm in the mood to flirt with anyone tonight."

"Then we'll just enjoy each other's company," I promised.

"That's right," Charlie agreed. "Who needs men?"

"Not us," Isabel declared. "They're nice and all, but we don't need them."

Davis raised his glass, offering a toast with his first real smile of the night. "Self-actualization, bitches!"

I laughed and drank to that, sinking into the warm comfort of my friends and the slight buzz from the decadently fizzy drink. Now that my photo ops with my dad were over, I could finally relax. It was his big night, and I'd done my part to show my support. The worst of my anxiety had passed when the journalists had moved on to take candids of the most fabulous, wealthy guests at this gala. I could unwind and have fun.

"So, Allie." Davis' attention fixed on me, his tone dropping to something more serious. "Are you going to tell us why you looked all bummed out and tired recently? Don't get me wrong, you look lovely tonight."

"Stunning." Isabel nodded.

"This gown is perfection on you," Charlie added, tilting her head at the softly iridescent, sage silk dress that draped over my modest curves in all the right places.

I gave her a wry smile. "Well, you picked it out. Thanks for all your help getting me ready for this fundraiser. And you guys." I included my other friends.

Davis waved up and down my body. "Honey, we had nothing to do with this hotness."

I beamed at them. "You all talked me down from the worst of my anxiety in the limo before we arrived. I couldn't have gotten through that photo op otherwise. My smile would've looked like a grimace. It wouldn't be the first time." I shuddered at memories of my most awkward years and how they'd been plastered all over the news every time my dad hosted a public event. Now the embarrassing pictures endured on the internet for everyone to see.

"This is what we're here for," Charlie declared.

"And the free Champagne," Davis amended.

"And these freaking delicious hors d'oeuvres. I am dying for the bacon-wrapped shrimp." Isabel popped another one in her mouth for effect, and her eyes rolled back in her head in a show of exaggerated ecstasy.

"But you were looking a little down before tonight." Davis wasn't willing to drop this.

Damn it. I couldn't breathe a word about Max or my confrontation with his awful sister.

"I was staying up late researching an old case." I settled on most of the truth. "It was really gruesome. I didn't get much sleep for a week or so because of some of the crime scene photos."

"Aw, babe." Isabel's long fingers wrapped around mine and offered a gentle, supportive squeeze. "Why didn't you tell us?"

I shrugged, resisting the urge to bite my lip. I hated lying to my friends, even if I was only skirting the worst of the truth. "I have to look at stuff like this for my job. I'm going to have to get used to it."

"But you don't have to do it alone," Charlie said sternly. "Talk to us next time. Or you don't have to talk about it at all; just call, and we'll come over with a bottle of pinot and a Disney film."

My heart swelled. "I love you guys so much."

"As much as you love the Beast?" Davis snickered.

My cheeks heated. "No," I groaned. "I never should've told you that I think the Beast is hotter in his beast form than as the Prince."

Isabel giggled. "I'm in total agreement. The prince is just meh. The Beast is all growly and possessive. It's so romantic."

"What happened to *self-actualization, bitches*?" Charlie asked. "Are we really going to romanticize your favorite childhood Stockholm syndrome movie?"

"*Beauty and the Beast* is not a Stockholm syndrome story!" Davis countered, exaggeratedly affronted. "He becomes a better man to deserve her because he loves her. And she falls in love with him for who he is on the inside."

Charlie snorted. "See? You do love love."

"Gaston is kind of hot, though." Isabel's voice took on a dreamy quality. "I know he's the baddie, but…yeah. He's hot."

Davis gaped at her. "Okay, honey. We're gonna to need to discuss this. Chauvinists are not hot."

"Totally not hot," I agreed with shocking vehemence. Max's dismissive eye roll flashed through my mind, and my fingers flexed as I remembered how the nickname *Bambi* sounded in his rumbling, deep voice.

"Yes!" Davis high-fived me. "Allie knows what's up."

"Um," Charlie began hesitantly, "I know you don't want to hear this, but I think your dad is waving for you to come over." Her cornflower blue eyes were apologetic.

I offered her a small smile. "It's not your fault. You guys don't drink all the Champagne without me.

And Isabel, I want to hear all the details about your audition yesterday. I'll be back soon."

I rubbed my thumb over the smooth back of my locket once before slipping on my composed mask and making my way through the crowd. My dad was talking to Mike and another middle-aged, dark haired man I vaguely recognized.

As I joined them, I recalled that his name was Mikhail Ivanov, a Russian billionaire who was one of my father's most important donors. An exceptionally tall man, he towered over Mike and had several inches of height on my dad. His hair was so densely black that I suspected a dye job, but it matched his close-cropped beard, so it might be natural. His dark eyes focused on me, thick lashes narrowing as he assessed me.

I wanted to flee in the face of his scrutiny, but I resolutely maintained my composure.

"There she is!" Mike beamed at me, and his eyes widened with something like relief. His tux was a little too tight around his belly, one of the buttons straining slightly. Next to the imposing Russian, he seemed far more human. I'd always thought of him as a larger-than-life personal hero. My heart tugged, and my steps quickened as I hastened to join my mentor in a show of solidarity.

Mikhail offered me a polite smile that didn't

quite reach his eyes. The man was notoriously calculating, an obscenely rich, billionaire businessman who'd worked his way to the top through ruthless acquisitions and international maneuvering. For a moment, the flash of his dark eyes reminded me of Francesca's shark-like, calculating gaze, and my steps faltered.

What else did your daddy tell you about his dirty dealings? Tell me everything you know about his relationship with the Russians. Max's deranged question echoed through my mind, and the memory of my time in his basement chilled my skin.

I shook my head slightly, as though I could forcibly rid myself of the thought. It was insane that I would even recall his words in this moment. Just because Mikhail Ivanov was Russian didn't make him a dangerous criminal. No matter how intimidating I found him, the billionaire businessman had a fearsome but respectable reputation. My father wouldn't associate with him if he was at all involved with the Bratva.

It was ludicrous to even consider otherwise. I'd looked at the evidence for myself; there was no Bratva involvement in the Five Families case. There were zero connections between my dad and Russian organized crime.

I focused on Mike, his need for help bolstering

my resolve. I straightened my spine and spread my lips in a practiced smile. When I attended these events for my father, I'd learned to slip into a different persona, drawing on my confident façade like a costume. Isabel had coached me using acting techniques, and I'd gotten pretty good at appearing poised when necessary. No matter how shaky I felt on the inside.

"Allie, I was just telling your dad about all the hard work you've been putting in at the office. Especially considering the extra time you've spent researching our old cases for your studies. Ron, you've raised a brilliant young woman."

My father's proud grin flooded my chest with warmth, and my own smile broadened with genuine delight. "That's my girl. Allie, you remember Mikhail Ivanov." He made sure to include one of his biggest donors in the conversation. "Mikhail, my daughter, Allie. She's interning at the US Attorney's Office this summer." His chest practically swelled with pride, and my eyes stung.

I blinked hard before the burst of emotion could crack my composed mask.

Mikhail nodded at me. "Yes, I remember." His Russian accent was still thick despite his years in America. "It's lovely to see you again, Allie."

"You too," I replied automatically. "And it's great

to see you, Mr. Callahan. I didn't realize you would be here tonight."

He clapped my dad on the shoulder. "Your old man was nice enough to extend an invite." He didn't tell me to call him Mike, and I was glad I hadn't. It seemed more appropriate to address him with professional courtesy in public, especially in front of important, intimidating men like Mikhail.

"You're studying your father's old cases?" The Russian shocked me by appearing interested. "Which ones? He had a very impressive career before finding his place in politics. It's why I've supported him for many years."

My cheeks heated at the sudden, intense attention. I'd expected to come over and snap a photo with Mikhail and then return to my friends. He'd never wanted to talk to me before.

But it only made sense for him to praise my dad. Especially when there was a journalist taking pictures nearby.

I took a breath and slipped deeper into my polished, charming persona: the confident woman who felt completely alien to me. "Yes, he's had an amazing career." I beamed at my dad. "Your work on the Five Families case was totally brilliant. No wonder crime rates are at an all-time low now that you're mayor."

My dad chuckled. "Flatterer."

"It's true," I asserted, rattling off crime statistics for the benefit of the hovering journalist. "You and Mr. Callahan were instrumental in dismantling the Mafia, and they haven't gained a foothold since."

"Why is a young woman like you spending all her time rehashing the past?" Mikhail questioned in an incisive tone I didn't care for. It took effort not to visibly bristle as he continued. "Surely, there's no need to go through records of such grisly crimes, when they happened so long ago."

"There's always something new to learn." Mike came to my defense, and I shot him a small, grateful smile. "Who knows? Allie might have fresh insight into some aspect of the case that we missed. In the future, she could use that in her own litigation. She has a very bright career ahead of her."

My heart swelled with gratitude and pride. "Thanks, Mr. Callahan."

Mikhail regarded me with those shark's eyes for a moment. "Yes, very impressive," he agreed in a monotone. "I'd like to introduce you to my son." He released me from his sharp gaze and searched the room. "Nikolai!" he called, beckoning.

Daddy laughed. Did it sound forced? "I'm sure the kids don't want to be set up by their parents."

My stomach dropped. *Oh, no.* Mikhail wanted

to set me up with his son? I didn't think I'd be able to remain composed if flirting was involved. I didn't even know how to flirt; I rarely went on dates, and I'd never had so much as a casual relationship. Living in my father's overprotective shadow, only a couple guys had worked up the courage to ask me out during my college years. I was pretty sure the mayor of New York had scared them off quickly. That, or it was just me and my social anxiety that made me too awkward to date.

This summer was supposed to be my opportunity to experiment and build my confidence with men. But I'd been so busy with my internship that I hadn't gotten a chance to practice dating.

My teeth sank into my lower lip, and I quickly pressed them together to stifle the nervous tic. I had no idea how to act charming around a guy my age, but I couldn't allow myself to appear awkward and standoffish in front of important donors.

I flexed and released my fingers at the small of my back, struggling to conceal the sudden tremor that manifested along with the spike of anxiety.

"Is there something wrong with my son?" Mikhail asked, his voice cold enough to frost our champagne glasses.

"Of course not," Daddy said quickly, his charismatic smile sliding firmly back into place. "He's a Harvard man, right? Very impressive."

"Yes," Mikhail replied, his tone still icy. "He just graduated and is now working at our family's organization."

"Another bright young person following in their father's footsteps," Mike interjected, coming in with the assist. His voice hitched slightly, but he still managed to support my dad despite how intimidated he was by Mikhail. He really was a great friend. "Allie, I'm sure you'll get along great."

It's not like I have to marry him, I told myself, struggling to calm the butterflies in my stomach. I could meet a guy and be polite to him, just like I would talk to any other important person at this event. It didn't matter if his dad wanted to set us up; I didn't have to go out with him. All I had to do was get through the next fifteen minutes or so before I could politely excuse myself and rejoin my friends.

"Niko." Daddy's gaze glinted at something over my shoulder. The hard warning in his eyes belied his broad, charming smile. "It's great to see you again."

I turned to face the Russian businessman's son, and for a moment, I forgot how to breathe. Nikolai Ivanov was stunning. His sable hair was effortlessly styled, pushed back off his brow to reveal the full impact of his perfectly masculine face. He was all hard planes and slightly rough edges, with designer stubble shadowing his square jaw. Aquamarine eyes glittered like gemstones, ringed in indigo that made them shine all the brighter. At well over six feet tall, he towered over me as he approached.

He might even be taller than Max. And judging by the way his tux fit close to his massive frame, he was every bit as heavily muscled as my dark stalker.

A shiver raced over my skin. Why was I thinking about Max? I had to focus on maintaining my composure. The last thing I needed was to think about the scarred, damaged man who'd kidnapped and interrogated me in his basement.

I shoved him from my mind and focused on Nikolai. It wasn't difficult; as he brushed against the edge of my personal space, his powerful, confident bearing practically pulsed over my flesh. His shockingly blue gaze swept my features, not dipping any lower than my modest sweetheart neckline. Despite the respectful appraisal, my skin tingled everywhere his eyes trailed over me.

I'd never enjoyed the attention of a man this beautiful, and my body was reacting strangely. My belly quivered, and something hot zinged down my spine to warm my insides.

"Nikolai, this is Allie." Mikhail introduced us. "She's Ron's daughter. She's a very impressive young woman, and I wanted you to meet." His voice dropped deeper on the last, ringing with command.

Oh, god. He really did want to set us up.

My stomach did a funny flip.

Nikolai extended his hand, and I accepted it automatically. Long, warm fingers engulfed mine in a gentle handshake. I returned it firmly, like my father had taught me, and a dazzling smile illuminated his features. "It's nice to meet you, Allie."

"You too." Was that my voice? It sounded far too breathless and weirdly husky.

"Allie is interning at the US Attorney's office," Mikhail continued. "Where do you attend college?" he asked me.

I realized I'd held on to Nikolai's hand for a second too long, and I snatched mine away, my cheeks heating. I turned back to his father, willing my features to arrange in a polite smile. I barely managed it.

"NYU," I supplied.

His thin lips quirked in a frown. "Not Ivy League?"

The slight disapproval in his tone helped wash away some of the weird jitteriness that'd fizzed through my veins. "No, I didn't want to go Ivy," I asserted evenly.

"It's Ron's alma mater," Mike interjected, providing more help.

I shot him a grateful glance, and I could've sworn his lashes twitched in the hint of a wink.

"Oh, yes." The furrow eased from Mikhail's brow. "I'd forgotten."

"My dad thinks Harvard is the only good university in the country," Nikolai explained. "I'm sure your resume must be very impressive if you secured an internship at the U.S. Attorney's office."

I turned my grateful smile on him. As soon as my eyes met his stunning blue gaze, my cheeks flushed with a rush of heat. He was so brilliantly beautiful that I could barely stand to look him in the eye. How was I going to stand here and make small talk for another fifteen minutes?

"Thanks," I managed to murmur, resisting the almost overwhelming urge to drop my gaze in shyness. "You went to Harvard?"

He shrugged, as though his prestigious degree meant little to him. "Yes, I just graduated. I'm thinking about getting my MBA next year, though. Maybe I'll apply at NYU." His grin hit me square in the chest.

"Don't joke, Nikolai," his father scolded, his voice heavy with disapproval. "You're working for the family business now. No need to waste another year on your education."

Nikolai's smile twitched ever so slightly, faltering. With annoyance? He'd clearly been needling his father with the NYU comment, but he didn't seem to like being censured in public.

I didn't blame him. I'd want to sink into the floor if my dad rebuked me in front of people I barely knew.

"Excuse me," a new, masculine voice cut into our conversation. "Could I get a photo, please?"

Oh, no. Now so wasn't a good time for a photo op. I was way too off balance for this moment to be permanently captured and potentially posted on the internet.

Nikolai cocked his head at me, those glimmering eyes quickly studying every nuance of my expression. The intense attention was riveting, and I stared up at him in stunned silence for a second, utterly entranced.

The heavy click of a camera jolted through my body like a firecracker, and I jumped slightly. A warm hand brushed my elbow, steadying me. The camera clicked again as I looked up at Nikolai in surprise at the casual touch. Heat sank into my skin where we made the lightest contact, and warmth flooded my stomach when I found myself locked in the glow of his heart-stopping smile. He was close enough for me to smell his cologne: something expensive that was an intoxicating combination of spice and tobacco and man.

I'd been on a total of five dates with boys before, and I'd been close enough to kiss two of them. But Nikolai wasn't a boy; he was an imposing man. No one had ever affected me this strongly, and he was barely touching me.

A memory of Max's big hands engulfing my calves burst across my mind, and I felt the phantom heat of his massive body as he leaned in close.

You don't have to be afraid of me, Bambi. I'm sorry if I scared you.

A small shiver ran through me. The camera clicked again, snapping me fully back to the present.

Nikolai was still watching me with that almost predatory focus, his eyes tracing the pebbled skin at my collarbones. "That's enough," he told the journalist, never taking his eyes off me.

I was peripherally aware that the cameraman left, but I couldn't tear my gaze from his. He was magnetic, and his intense attention captivated me completely. I'd never experienced anything like it. It was unnerving, but it set off all my feminine gratification signals. The warmth that bloomed in my chest was heady, a pleasant sensation I'd never felt before.

"Hey, Allie." Isabel's melodic voice wrapped around me, tugging my attention away from him. "We're missing you over by the chocolate fountain."

I turned to her, grateful for the lifeline. My protective friend must've noticed my discomfiture and come to my rescue.

"There's a chocolate fountain?" My voice squeaked slightly, increasing the burning heat in my cheeks. I was probably red all the way to my ears by now. No amount of makeup in the world could conceal a flush this intense. Damn my pale complexion.

She wrapped my hand in hers, lacing our fingers together. Isabel really was better than any big sister I ever could've asked for. I returned her gentle squeeze, a silent *thank you.*

"Will you excuse us, Mr. Fitzgerald?" she asked, all charm and grace. "Allie needs sustenance."

My dad laughed, a rich, warm sound. He'd always liked Isabel. I was pretty sure he approved of her protectiveness. "I'm not sure if chocolate counts as sustenance."

"There are strawberries," Isabel countered. "Totally healthy."

"Totally," he agreed, chuckling. "Go on." He

waved toward the fountain, giving me an out. "Have fun, sweetheart."

Isabel tugged on my hand, leading me away from the anxiety-inducing conversation and the mind-scrambling, handsome man who'd cracked my composed mask.

"Oh my god, he's so hot," Isabel said in an undertone as she led me away. "Are you sure you want to be rescued? You seemed shaken, but OMG. That man is sex on a stick."

My giggle was slightly manic. "He's way too hot for me. I could barely look at him! Thanks for coming to get me. I think his dad wanted to set us up. It was really uncomfortable."

Isabel stopped in her tracks. "Wait, wait. You actually have an opportunity to date that man candy? We're going back."

I dug in my heels. "No!" I hissed. "He's too beautiful. I couldn't handle it."

I could still feel the phantom heat of his hand on my arm. And for some reason, I sensed the lingering caress of Max's touch on my legs.

I shook my head to clear it. The fact that I was thinking about Max was a total red flag. If Nikolai intimidated me as much as my stalker, that wasn't a good basis for a relationship.

I needed to put both men firmly out of my mind.

They were clearly dangerous for me in different ways. Nikolai was tempting and impossibly gorgeous, whereas Max was... I didn't really have words for how Max made me feel. There were too many conflicting emotions where he was concerned: fear, anger, pity, gratitude.

My stomach flipped, and I took a decisive step toward the chocolate fountain. "I need sugar," I announced, imbuing my voice with as much confidence as I could muster.

Isabel sighed. "Don't we all?"

She clearly didn't approve of the fact that I was running away from a man as appealing as Nikolai, but my friend was loyal to her core. If I didn't want to think about darkly imposing men, she would distract me.

And I definitely didn't want to think about Nikolai or Max.

CHAPTER 12

"Are you sure you don't want us to stay for a little while longer?" Charlie asked, her cornflower blue eyes soft with concern.

My friends waited beside their limo, hesitating to get in and abandon me.

"I'll be okay," I promised. "Daddy said he's making his final goodbyes. Most of the guests have left already, anyway. I promised I'd catch a ride home with him."

"But why aren't you riding with us?" Davis asked with an exaggerated pout. "We all came here together. We deserve a little more limo time."

I laughed and waved them into the waiting car. "You guys enjoy as much limo time as you want. I think my dad wants to check in with me. I was seriously awkward around the Ivanovs. He's probably worried that I'm upset. You know how protective he is."

Isabel offered me an understanding smile and opened the door, ushering the other two inside. "I know it's probably taken all of his restraint to stop himself from constantly checking in on you this summer. We totally get it. If he needs to talk to you tonight so that you can keep living your fabulous, independent life with us, then that's okay. We need you to be able to come out with us whenever you want."

She pulled me into a tight hug, and I returned it with a fierce squeeze. "Thank you."

"Anytime," she promised. "We've got your back." She disengaged and joined the others in the limo. After the door closed, they rolled down the window so they could wave at me as they pulled away. I heard the distinctive pop of a champagne cork, and Davis let out a whoop of excitement.

My heart tugged toward them, but my smile stayed in place as I waved after them. Isabel understood. I needed to talk to my dad if I wanted to maintain my freedom.

Even if that freedom did come along with a dark stalker.

The phantom feel of Max's strong arms closing around me as he pulled me out of the way of the oncoming car drew a shiver to the surface of my skin.

He's not stalking me anymore, I reminded myself. I hadn't seen so much as a glimpse of him since he'd walked away from me three days ago, returning to his sister for verbal torment.

My chest squeezed. No matter how unstable he was, Max didn't deserve her cruelty. Those caustic remarks about his accident probably were a contributing factor to his madness. I still couldn't understand why he would risk kidnapping me for her sake. He must be very close with his father.

His father, the infamous mobster who'd been sent to prison by my dad.

Sometimes love is hard, but blood is everything. The memory of his tragic declaration made my heart twist. Love shouldn't be hard.

"Are you cold?" I jolted at the close proximity of the deep, masculine voice. A large, warm hand touched my shoulder, steadying me. "Sorry, I didn't mean to startle you."

I realized I'd hugged my arms close to my aching chest while I'd been thinking about Max and his awful family. And I recognized the heat of that casual touch.

Nikolai Ivanov stood just at the edge of my personal space: a respectful but intimate distance. I had to crane my neck back to meet his eyes. His sheer size and that striking blue gaze stunned me all over again.

"Here," he offered, unbuttoning his jacket. "If you're waiting for you dad, there's no need for you to stand here shivering." He draped the garment over my shoulders before I could formulate a coherent sentence. It was warm from his body heat, and it smelled like his intoxicating cologne.

"You don't have to do that, Nikolai," I protested, even though he was already withdrawing those big, masculine hands, leaving me huddled in his huge jacket.

The midnight breeze was barely chilly on this summer night, and I really hadn't been cold.

His sensual lips twisted in a cocky smile. "It's Niko. And I know I didn't have to. But it gives me an excuse to talk to you. Now, you can't try to run away again." He fingered the lapel, just over my collarbone. "Not unless you want to steal my jacket, which would be a shame."

I gaped at him, my brain scrambled by that smile.

Was this flirting? I didn't know how to do it. Maybe he was just being nice.

"I didn't get a chance to ask you out before your friend came and stole you away," he remarked, trailing long fingers down my arm as he pulled away.

The silky glide of his jacket beneath his fingertips teased my skin, and my senses jumped to attention. Something quivered in my belly, and I barely resisted the urge to squirm beneath his intense stare. His pale eyes glittered, and that tilted smile was sharp enough to cut through all my rational thoughts.

Before I could formulate a response, something massive and dark burst from the shadows and collided with Niko.

"Get away from her." My stomach dropped at the familiar, rough growl.

Max. Oh my god, Max was here. And he'd shoved Niko away from me.

He stood between us, his massive shoulders rippling beneath his tight black shirt. I couldn't see his face, but the memory of his fearsome, twisted snarl as he'd interrogated me flashed across my mind.

Niko's handsome face was blank for a moment, his cocky smile knocked away by shock. Then, his brows drew low over those stunning eyes, and his white teeth flashed in a snarl of his own. "Back off if you know what's good for you." He took a threatening step toward us, and Max's body swelled with barely leashed violence.

"Stop!" I gasped, the plea popping out before my

mind could fully process what was happening. Instinctively, I knew that two predators were about to rip into each other, and I couldn't allow that to happen. "Max, stop!"

He stiffened, his entire body seizing up as thought I'd hit him with a bolt of electricity. He didn't turn to face me, but he didn't advance on Niko, either.

"Get out of here, Bambi," he ordered, his voice deep and fierce.

Acting on pure instinct, I reached out and grasped his shoulder, as though I could physically restrain him. His muscles flexed beneath my fingers, all that power coiled tight and ready to explode. I knew it wouldn't be directed at me if he did unleash his worst urges.

I was so close to Max now that I couldn't see Niko past the bulk of his body. His chest expanded on deep, rapid breaths, as though he'd just run a mile. Had he exerted himself racing to get to Niko? Or was the enormous effort to hold himself back causing him physical strain?

He'd snapped at Niko to get away from me. He'd shoved us apart and put himself between us.

Whatever insanity was going on in his mind, I sensed that he thought he was protecting me again.

It was dangerous for Max to be here. For his

sake, no one should know that we were remotely connected. And he shouldn't be anywhere near my father.

Oh, god. Was that why he was here? Was he surveilling my dad as part of his crazy vendetta?

"You need to leave, Max." My voice came out firm and even, the need to protect my father—and to save Max from himself—overriding my confusion at the sudden, shocking turn of events.

"I'm not leaving you alone with him." The refusal was gravelly with a harsh threat, and he didn't take his eyes off Niko.

"Seriously, you need to go," I said with more urgency. Out of the corner of my eye, I spotted a bouncer leaving his post at the door and coming to check on the altercation. I squeezed his shoulder as hard as I could, commanding his attention. It probably felt like a light massage to him, judging by the mass of muscle in my grip. He practically vibrated beneath my touch, as though straining to resist an anchor's weight.

The bouncer would get to us within seconds.

I stepped around Max, blocking his path to Niko. A tremor raced through me when I looked into his fearsome expression. His full lips were peeled back from his teeth as he glowered at Niko, and he'd pushed his hair back from his brow. The

172

full extent of the damage to his face was on menacing display.

But it wasn't his scar, the mark of his pain, that made my knees weak. It was the white-hot flames that flickered over his black eyes. Hatred burned in their inky depths, the full force of his terrible rage directed at Niko.

He thinks he's defending me, I reminded myself. It didn't make any sense, but he'd put himself between Niko and me as though the handsome, flirtatious man was some sort of threat.

But Niko wasn't an oncoming car, and I didn't need rescuing. His father was one of my father's most generous donors, and there would be hell to pay if Max punched Mikhail Ivanov's son. Max would be arrested for assault at the very least. And that was if his misguided vendetta against my dad didn't come to light. If anyone found out that he'd been stalking Ron Fitzgerald at his big fundraising event, Max would definitely serve jail time.

But I knew that Max didn't need to be punished; he needed help.

And he'd saved my life. I owed him for that, no matter what else he'd done to me.

"Max," I said his name more gently.

Those black eyes snapped to mine, singeing me with the heat of his hatred. A shudder ran down my spine, and he blinked. The terrifying flames in his dark gaze extinguished, and his snarl eased slightly. His sharp features remained tight with strain, but I recognized the ferocious disapproval in the tension around his jaw. He'd looked at me like this after he'd pulled me out of the path of that car: pissed at me for risking my life, but not enraged.

"You need to leave." I kept my tone gentle, coaxing him to listen. "We can talk later, okay?" I meant it. We needed to have another conversation about his insane, vengeful mission against my dad. I'd thought that I could leave him to it, that he'd eventually come to a dead end and drop this madness.

But it seemed he was just as unstable as ever, and he'd get himself caught if he didn't see reason. He'd clearly suffered enough, and continuing his vendetta would only cause him more pain in the end. I had to convince him to let go of this rage, or it would eat away at what was left of his sanity.

"What's going on here?" The bouncer had arrived. "Are you okay, Mr. Ivanov?"

Max's eyes snapped back to Niko, glowering at him over my shoulder. I placed my hand flat against his chest, as though that would be enough to restrain him if he went for Niko again.

"You have to go now, Max." Every time I said his

name, he seemed more inclined to listen. On the night he'd kidnapped me, I'd used it in order to connect us on a more human level. The imprint of that harrowing experience seemed to have stuck, because he didn't lunge for Niko. His heart hammered beneath my palm, and sweat beaded on his ruined brow.

His dark gaze found mine again, and the hateful flames guttered and died. "We'll discuss this later." It was a dark promise.

A shiver danced over my skin, but I didn't shrink away. "Okay." I dropped my voice lower. "Meet me at my place. Outside," I added firmly. No matter how much I wanted to help him, I didn't think I could bear it if I stepped into my sanctuary and found my kidnapper waiting in the shadows.

His jaw ticked, but he offered me a tight nod and stepped back sharply, severing the connection between us. He shot one last warning glower at Niko before turning on his heel and stalking away.

I spun to face the bouncer. "Everything's fine," I told him, my tone a little too high-pitched. I searched for Niko's blue gaze, unsure how I would explain this away. "Sorry about that."

Niko's brows were still drawn low over his eyes, but he wasn't snarling anymore. "You know him?" he demanded.

I flinched, but I forced myself to hold my ground. "Yeah. We, um, know each other from school," I lied frantically. "I guess he was passing by and misinterpreted the situation."

It was a completely ridiculous explanation, but it was all I could think of on the spot. Niko's taut expression didn't ease.

Crap. I was a terrible liar.

"Sorry," I said again, at a loss.

He shook his head slightly, and the harshest edges of his handsome face softened. "It's not your fault," he assured me. His expression softened further, the sensual curve returning to his lips. "Are you okay?"

"Yeah." Damn it, my voice shook. I swallowed and tried again. "Yeah, that was just kind of intense."

"Are you sure you're all right, Miss Fitzgerald?" The bouncer looked at me skeptically, as though he could tell I was lying, too.

"Yes!" I had to get out of here before someone told my dad about this. He'd forcibly drag me back home if he had to. I couldn't live like that anymore, no matter how much I loved him.

I shrugged out of Niko's jacket and handed it back to him. "I have to go. Please don't tell my dad about this? He'll worry, and there's nothing to worry about."

The bouncer nodded, agreeable to do as I asked. "Of course, Miss Fitzgerald. Should I get you a cab?"

"Yes, please." I practically sagged with relief, but I forced my spine to remain straight.

"That man is dangerous," Niko warned. His eyes glinted, and his jaw firmed.

The white knight clearly wasn't ready to let this go. He was impossibly gorgeous and protective. I should be swooning all over him, but I was anxious to get home and talk to Max.

"I know he looks scary, but he's not a threat to me," I said honestly. "I really think he believed he was defending me. It was totally uncalled for, and I'm sorry he shoved you like that."

A shadow ticked along his jaw, but his eyes remained soft on my face. "You should stay away from him."

"Yeah," I agreed, making no promises. Anyone with half a brain could see that I should stay away from Max. That didn't mean I was going to. There was too much a stake now for me to ignore him entirely.

My taxi pulled up, and the bouncer opened the door for me.

"Thanks." I made sure to direct my gratitude at Niko as well. He only had the best intentions, and I truly did appreciate that he cared about my safety. "I'm fine," I promised. "Goodnight."

I didn't wait to see what else Niko might say before I closed the door and gave the driver my address. I couldn't give him the opportunity to continue questioning me about how I knew Max, and I didn't want to bump into my father as he exited the building. My emotions were a frazzled mess, and my dad would definitely pick up on my distress if he got one look at my face.

I pulled out my phone and texted him my excuses, saying that I was tired and had gotten a cab. Max and my father didn't belong anywhere near each other, and the sooner I could convince Max of that fact, the better.

I took a deep breath and flexed my shaking fingers in an attempt to siphon off some of my jittery energy. In a few minutes, I would have to face Max again. Arguing with him was like shouting at an enraged bull. It would take all my resolve and wits to convince him to abandon his vendetta.

CHAPTER 13

ALLIE

*H*e was waiting for me when I stepped out of the cab: a dark shadow lurking on my front porch. My stomach flipped, but I resolutely walked toward him.

I am strong. I am independent. I can do this.

I had to see this through, for his sake. I no longer believed he was a threat to my dad; there was no conspiracy for him to uncover. But if he continued stalking my family, he would eventually be caught.

I remembered his sister's cruel taunts. I didn't know exactly what he'd been through, but Max had suffered enough. The pain he must've experienced when he was branded with that awful scar must have been excruciating. And now he would forever carry the mark of that pain, unable to hide the severity of his trauma, no matter how much he might want to.

I didn't know much about Max, but my few intense encounters with him suggested that he abhorred weakness. He'd scorned my pity, and he'd been at his most unstable when I betrayed a hint of sympathy.

Max had been beautiful once. Now he believed he was a monster. And I suspected that for all his warnings about dangerous men in organized crime, his monster lived on the surface of his skin, not in his soul.

I squared my shoulders, resolute. As I approached, Max straightened from his casual pose where he'd been leaning against my front door. He moved closer to the streetlight, so the illumination caught on his sharp cheekbones and jaw. That skull-like mask had terrified me in the basement. Now, I knew what lurked underneath: a damaged man who preferred to hide in shadow rather than expose the mark of his pain to the world. He'd rather frighten people away than let them get close enough to see his scarred face.

But I'd been close enough. Not only had I seen the scar on his flesh, but I'd watched his awful sister inflict deep wounds with her cutting remarks. How many times had she slashed him with her sharp tongue? Max had said that she'd served as his legal guardian for five years. His mother had been dead and his father imprisoned. My heart ached to think about an abandoned, tormented teenage Max living in that grand house with rot at its core.

Had he been scarred even then? How long had she been tearing into him with that particular emotional lash?

He must love his father very much to put himself at such risk to defend his family from the false threat posed by my dad.

I lifted my chin and joined him on the stoop, meeting him squarely in the eye. The streetlight flashed over the black pools, tiny pinpoints of light in a sea of darkness.

"Sorry if I scared you." His voice was a deep, soothing rumble, as though he was speaking to a spooked doe.

I'd thought *Bambi* was a derisive nickname, but maybe there was more to it. I still believed that he was keeping an emotional barrier between us, but he'd also protected me. He'd saved me from being hit by that car and insisted on seeing me safely to my door. Even though his actions tonight had been deranged, he'd thought he was defending me.

We needed to sort this out right now.

"You didn't scare me," I replied honestly. "I'm scared for you."

He drew back ever so slightly, as though I'd

shoved the brick wall of his hard chest. "Nikolai Ivanov doesn't scare me." It was a rough growl.

I blew out a sigh. "Yeah, I kind of got that from how you were snarling at him." I gestured to the concrete step in front of my house. "Can we talk?"

He lifted a brow in challenge. "Don't want me to come inside?" The sneer that tilted his lips let me know that he fully understood why I didn't want him in my sanctuary: the last time he'd been in my home, he'd drugged and kidnapped me.

I fixed him with a cool stare and sat down on the step, waiting for him to join me.

He let out a sigh of his own and settled down beside me, his big body moving with predatory grace. Suddenly, an image of a panther slid through my mind: sleek and powerful, with sharp teeth that could tear apart anyone who threatened him.

The beast was a rest now, his shoulders relaxing. A shiver raced over my skin, and he frowned.

Before I could formulate my first argument against his continued vendetta, he shrugged out of his leather jacket and draped it over my shoulders.

"You don't have to do that," I protested, even as I was enveloped by the warmth of his residual body heat. Unlike Niko's tux, Max's jacket didn't smell like expensive cologne. The earthy scent of the leather mingled with something deeper that was purely masculine and uniquely *Max*.

"I do if you insist on sitting outside," he retorted. "That dress sure as hell won't keep you warm."

My blush descended all the way down my chest, further heating my skin. It suddenly felt far too revealing, and I wrapped Max's jacket more tightly around me to hide the redness that colored my pale skin. I didn't want my body to betray the fact that he'd elicited such a strong reaction with his single, incisive remark.

He shifted again, reaching for something behind him. He pulled out a brown paper bag that had the distinct shape of a wine bottle.

"Here." He handed it to me, but I didn't take it right away.

"What's this?"

He rolled his eyes at me in that infuriating way. "It's wine."

Irritation prickled my spine. "Yeah, I can see that. Why do you have wine?"

He shrugged. "I thought I scared you back there. I figured I'd bring it as an apology. You don't have to be afraid of me."

"I'm not," I promised, reaching for the bottle.

Before I could take it from him, his long fingers

deftly unscrewed the cap with a definitive clicking noise.

"There. Now you know it's not poisoned." One corner of his lips twitched, and the light danced over his eyes.

"That's not funny," I retorted, waiting for the shudder of residual fear at his reference to my time in his basement. But the signs of terror didn't come. All I felt was that hot, prickling irritation, and before I could think better of it, I snatched the bottle and took a swig of the wine in an act of defiance.

You don't scare me.

The heated needling sensation melted into a flood of warmth at the rich flavor of the pinot noir. It was smooth, fruity, and comforting. Not as nice as my favorite vintage that I kept in my wine rack, but close enough.

I lowered the bottle and briefly unsheathed it from the paper bag to inspect the label. My taste-buds had been right: pinot noir.

"How did you know I like pinot?"

His expression went carefully blank, and he shrugged again. "Educated guess."

Oh. He'd been in my apartment. He'd probably gone through my things, looking for nonexistent evidence to use against my father.

The shudder of revulsion finally rolled through

my body. I hated that he'd violated the privacy of my home, the place where I was supposed to find strength and independence.

He snagged the bottle from my hand, lifted it to his lips, and took a long gulp. His throat worked as he swallowed, drinking way too fast.

"Hey." I placed my fingers on his wrist to direct the bottle away from his mouth. "Don't get drunk. I need to talk to you."

He lowered the wine with a grimace. "This isn't nearly strong enough to make me drunk."

I snatched the wine from him, moving it safely away from his grasp. I set it on the step on my opposite side, ensuring it wasn't within easy reach. I needed him to focus.

"About tonight," I began, settling back into calm purpose. "You can't keep stalking my dad like this. I know I said it didn't matter to me, but it does. You're going to get caught. Especially if you do something as stupid as attacking Mikhail Ivanov's son in plain view of event security. If my father had already been outside, he would've gone ballistic."

Max's jaw tightened, taking on the harsh line I was starting to recognize all too well: he was pissed that I'd supposedly put myself in danger. "But he wasn't outside, was he, Bambi? You were standing there with the son of a Russian oligarch, with no regard for your safety. Nikolai is dangerous. You shouldn't be anywhere near him."

"That's funny," I said coolly. "He said the same thing about you."

"Of course he did," Max bit back. "That's because I am dangerous. You just don't want to believe it."

The hot prickling of my annoyance spread from my spine all the way to my fingers and toes. His matching irritation rolled off him and collided with mine. Sparks pinged over my skin, making every inch of my body come alive.

"Yes, I get it. You're so menacing and brooding." I gave him an eye roll of my own. "You would've torn Niko apart. That doesn't mean you pose a threat to me. I understand that now."

"*Niko?*" His voice deepened to something dark and rough. "You're close with that monster?"

I scoffed. "He's just a man, Max. An obscenely wealthy but normal man. And no, we're not close. I only met him tonight." Something clicked into place in my mind. "Wait, you hate him because he's Russian? Is that what this is about? Your prejudice?"

"It's not prejudice," he growled. "You just don't want to know the truth. And I don't want you to know it, either. I told you not to keep digging into your father's case against my family, and I meant it.

Why was *Niko* getting close to you tonight? Does his family know about your little investigation?"

My cheeks flamed with something indefinable. Anger? Embarrassment?

"He was asking me out before you came and shoved him away," I retorted. "Is that so hard to believe? That he's interested in me like a normal guy is interested in a girl? This isn't some conspiracy, Max."

"Of course it's not hard to believe," he snapped back, as though I'd offended *him* somehow. "You're beautiful and intelligent, and your father is the mayor of New York. That's why it's so convenient for his father to task him with keeping an eye on you."

I shook my head in disbelief, momentarily struck dumb by the depth of his delusion.

"Do they know about your investigation or not?" he barreled on, every bit the charging, rage-blinded bull.

"No, they don't." I struggled to keep the lie from my tone. Mike had boasted about my interest in the Five Families case in front of Mikhail, but that had to be pure coincidence. If I admitted it to Max, it would just reinforce his insane beliefs.

His dark eyes narrowed. "You'd better hope they don't. Stay away from Nikolai Ivanov."

"You can't tell me what to do!" I declared, indignant. How dare he tell me who I could and couldn't date?

He leaned toward me, imposing the full weight of his menace. His sensual lips thinned as he hissed a warning, "I can, and I will. You don't want to believe there are monsters around you, even when they're in plain view. Nikolai might look pretty, but he's every bit as monstrous as I am."

I pushed into the heat of his anger, my burning frustration mingling with his. "Well, guess what, Max? I don't think you're a monster at all. I think—"

"Stop talking, Bambi." The low command was hot against my lips, his barely contained rage and pain teasing over my skin in a tingling wave.

"I told you not to call me Bambi," I hissed right back. "You can't tell me who to date, and you can't tell me what to believe. You might not like it, but I've seen you, Max. You're not a monster. You're—"

My tirade was smothered when his mouth clashed with mine. For a moment, I froze, stunned by his heat and raw ferocity. The low growl that made my belly quiver rumbled against my lips, hungry rather than enraged.

Shocked, I sucked in a gasp, and his lips molded to mine. The heat of my frustration turned molten, rolling down my spine like warm honey. My hands lifted to his chest, but when I touched the hard, rippling wall of muscle, I didn't push him away. My fingers twined in his shirt, clinging on to him for support as my head began to spin.

The kiss was feverish and rough, our battle of wills descending into something purely primal and fierce. His tongue, which had issued so many sharp retorts and scathing rebukes, surged into my mouth, seeking to tame mine. I met him with ferocity of my own, refusing to give him an inch.

My mind went hazy, anger morphing into raw aggression I'd never felt before. It had a ragged edge of need and hunger that drove me to a frenzy. One of his huge hands cupped my nape, his fingers sliding into my hair to trap me in place. He deepened the kiss, seeking control.

Suddenly, my fingernails were biting into his corded arms, and my teeth nipped at his sensual lips. He let out a purely masculine sound that rumbled straight through me to quiver in my core. Something pulsed inside me, and my need turned into a greedy craving for more. I'd lost track of where I was, *who* I was. My senses were entirely consumed by the feel of his tongue against mine, his salt-kissed leather scent, and the low, hungry sounds we exchanged on each ragged breath we shared.

Keeping one hand in my hair, his strong arm was

an iron band around the small of my back, pulling me closer and caging me. The heat that pulsed deep inside me surged, and I melted against him. Whatever wild, primal thing inside me that had driven me to this fierce madness finally surrendered to his strength and masculine will. Giddiness fizzed through my veins, crackling through my body. I allowed myself to drown in it, becoming drunk on the heady rush of his ruthless kiss. I opened for him, allowing him to claim me more deeply.

He groaned against me, taking everything I offered and demanding more. My head spun, and my fingers tingled where they curled into his flexing muscles. Finally, he pulled back, allowing me to breathe. I swayed toward him, not ready to end this thrilling madness that we shared. I didn't want to think; all I wanted was to feel his mouth on mine, his strength locking me exactly where he desired.

His fingers tightened in my hair, and little sparks of awareness danced over my scalp as he restrained me from demanding more. His forehead rested on mine, our lips so close that the pulsing inside me intensified to an aching throb.

"Allie…" He rasped my name, and I shivered at the feel of it sliding over my skin in a hot wave of need.

I leaned into him as much as his grip on my hair

would allow, and my brow brushed over his. The odd sensation of his too-smooth, scarred skin barely registered; I wanted his mouth on mine again, and I didn't care about his scar. Thinking about the mark of his pain made my heart clench, and my hands left his arms to clutch his shoulders. I might as well have tried to pull a granite statue closer.

As soon as his ruined brow touched mine, he stiffened in my hold. After a heartbeat of stony stillness, he recoiled from me as though I'd burned him. His strong arms released me, and he wrenched himself from my much weaker grasp as he surged to his feet.

I swayed, shaky in the wake of our intense kiss and his abrupt withdrawal. One big hand closed over my shoulder, steadying me for a moment. He jerked away almost immediately, reeling back and crossing his arms over his chest. I stared up at him, my jaw slack with shock.

He towered over me, a dark shadow. Every muscle in his massive body seemed to have locked up, and his face was twisted in a horrific scowl. He glowered at me, and white flames flickered over his black eyes.

"Max?" My voice was small, and he flinched at the sound of his name on my tongue.

"Go inside," he bit out.

I blinked rapidly, struggling to get my brain to work in the aftermath of his decimating kiss. "But—"

"Now," he snapped.

I wasn't sure what I intended to protest, but the whip of his command jolted me to my feet. His jacket slid off my shoulders, and he caught if before it hit the ground. I fumbled for my keys in my clutch, and I braced one hand on my door to steady myself. Max didn't offer me support this time.

My stomach dropped to the pavement, and I didn't understand why. The giddiness that'd flooded me sparked into jitters, leaving my fingers trembling and my mind an addled mess. For some reason, my lungs tightened, and my eyes stung. The molten honey that'd pooled in my belly soured, making my insides squirm.

Max's dark presence at my back teased over my skin like a physical touch, drawing a shudder from my chest. I couldn't bear to look at him. My neck locked up tight, refusing to turn and face him. All the hot defiance that'd driven me to a frenzy cooled to an icy chill, and my flesh pebbled.

My key finally turned the lock, and I bolted into the sanctuary of my home. Automatically, I slid the deadbolt into place behind me before lurching forward. I moved through my foyer and into my living room as though drunk, stumbling slightly as I kicked off my high heels.

I glanced out the huge bay window, my eyes drawn as though by a magnet. My dark protector was gone. Max had melted into the shadows, disappearing into the night.

CHAPTER 14

The woolen material of the ski mask stretched weirdly over my scar, teasing the live nerves at the edges of the damaged flesh. The constant contact with my sensory-deadened skin was a distracting, maddening reminder of how I hadn't been able to feel Allie's softness when she'd pressed her forehead to mine.

I'd been utterly consumed by the heat of our kiss, but that gut-wrenching reminder of my scar had poisoned the chemistry we shared. The mark of my shame reminded me of my duty.

Allie thought she could convince me to drop my vendetta against her father, but that would never happen.

I wanted her so fucking badly it set my teeth on edge, and I was a bastard for kissing her when I knew that I'd never allow her dad to escape my retribution.

I've seen you, Max. You're not a monster. A shudder rolled through my body at the memory of her heated declaration, and for an insane moment, I wanted to believe it.

I'd protect Allie. I'd saved her life and watched over her. Tonight, I'd been stalking Fitzgerald's fundraising event because three of my targets had been in attendance: Kelvin McCrae, Mikhail Ivanov, and Ron Fitzgerald himself.

But I'd witnessed that bastard, Nikolai, touching Allie, and I'd seen red. I couldn't quite recall what'd happened in the minute it'd taken me to get to them, to shove the Russian scum away from her. All I'd known was that I had to keep his filthy hands off her.

If she hadn't stopped me, I would've beaten his pretty face to a bloody pulp for daring to touch her.

I could still feel the warmth of her small hand at the center of my chest, that delicate touch halting me from advancing on my hated rival.

I flexed my fingers, struggling to let go of the tension that still lingered in my muscles. I'd craved to end him, but her quiet strength had restrained my worst impulses.

She was right: I would've been fucked if I'd snapped

in public and attacked Nikolai Ivanov. In a way, Allie had saved me tonight, just as much as I'd saved her.

I shook my head to clear it, and the damn ski mask rubbed over my scar again. I barely managed to bite back a growl. If I made a sound now, I'd blow my whole plan to hell. I'd end up in jail or dead.

Kelvin McCrae's beachfront mansion in the Hamptons was obscenely large, dark and cavernous at this time of night—well, morning. My encounter with Allie had thrown off my schedule by several hours. I'd almost missed my carefully planned shot at McCrae just to steal a kiss from her.

I rubbed the back of my neck, frustrated. I had to stop thinking about her, about that sizzling kiss. The best kiss of my life.

McCrae was mere steps away from me, and I had to focus. I'd managed to sneak past his security, and in a few more minutes, I'd get the evidence Kirill had told me about. McCrae had some kind of records about the night Allie's mom had died, and Fitzgerald had asked him to cover them up. I'd already started to put together what might've really happened to Marie Fitzgerald, but I needed the documents McCrae had saved as personal insurance against his *friend*, the mayor. I needed proof.

I stalked into McCrae's darkened bedroom. It

took me a second to realize that the rumbling snores were coming from his wife, not him. She'd been visibly inebriated by the end of the gala, and clearly, she'd passed out once she got home.

One less thing for me to worry about. If I could avoid disturbing her, I wouldn't have to deal with mitigating her screams. I had no intention of hurting Mrs. McCrae—she was innocent—but I'd been prepared to intimidate her into remaining silent while I dealt with her husband.

It seemed that she could be spared from the ordeal altogether.

Good.

I loomed over McCrae, moving as silently as a shadow. My gloved hand clamped over his mouth at the same time as the cold barrel of my gun kissed the spot directly between his eyes.

He jerked awake, and I applied pressure to force him to stillness.

"Don't make a sound." My low tone ghosted around us, but his adrenaline-sharpened senses ensured that he heard every word.

The whites of his eyes glowed in the darkness, and his head moved the tiniest fraction as he nodded his agreement.

I removed my hand from his mouth and eased to

the side, giving him room to stand without withdrawing the threat of my gun.

"You have evidence of what really happened on the night Ron Fitzgerald's wife died. You're going to give it to me."

His mouth opened and closed a few times like a fish out of water, gasping for life.

"The files are on my private server," he managed to wheeze. "In my office. Down the hall."

I tipped my head toward the bedroom door, never taking my eyes off him. "Let's go."

I kept my gun to his head as we slowly and silently stepped down the carpeted hall to his office. The house was dark and quiet; I hadn't done anything to alert security, and if McCrae tried anything, I would end him and get the hell out of here.

But I needed this evidence. I didn't know exactly what he'd been hiding away on his private server for a decade, but it was the first real lead I'd ever found to prove that Fitzgerald was corrupt.

Anticipation fizzed through my veins, and I had to focus to keep my hand from trembling around my gun. I swallowed the flutter of vindictive excitement and urged McCrae into his office, schooling my features to a carefully blank expression.

I'd worn the mask to conceal my identity, and I

didn't intend to use my fearsome scar to intimidate him. If all went according to plan, I'd leave him alive and mostly unharmed once he gave me what I wanted. McCrae was too important for me to kill him; the investigation would be rigorous and relentless if he were murdered.

So, I couldn't risk anyone glimpsing me tonight and learning my identity, least of all him.

I kept him at gunpoint as he collapsed into his office chair, his shaky knees giving out. His hand trembled as he started up his computer, and I edged farther back into the shadows, away from the blue light cast by the screen.

When McCrae entered his password and accessed the files, I tossed a flash drive onto his desk.

"I want a copy. Tell me what this has to do with Fitzgerald's ties to the Bratva."

"N-not the Bratva. The Mafia. It's all right there!" he squeaked, desperate when I lifted my gun from his heart to his skull. "It's the medical examiner's report on Marie's autopsy and the results of the arson investigation. Ron asked me to make them disappear, and I did. That's all I have, I swear."

I narrowed my eyes at him. "Explain."

When he babbled the significance of the files, my heart should've soared with triumph. I finally had some proof of Fitzgerald's corruption, even if it wasn't evidence of his ties to the Bratva.

Instead, something crumbled at the center of my chest as the full weight of the awful truth settled in my soul.

Allie could never know. It would break her. And if she found out the terrible facts of what'd really happened on the night of the fire, she'd never allow me to touch her again.

I had to keep an eye on her now that I knew the Ivanovs were interested in her. She'd claimed that they knew nothing about her reckless investigation into the case against my family, but I didn't believe her.

Watching her from a distance but not allowing myself close enough to touch her was going to be pure torture, but I would protect her, no matter what it cost me.

And she would never learn what I'd found out tonight.

CHAPTER 15

ALLIE

I'm as crazy as Max. I had to be, because I'd kissed my stalker. I'd kissed the man who was intent on blackmailing my dad.

I'd barely slept last night, unable to get comfortable. That strange heat persisted low in my belly, but my skin had been icy. Ever since Max had abruptly pushed me away, I'd been on the verge of tears whenever I thought about him.

And I couldn't stop thinking about him. About our kiss. The best kiss of my life.

Not that there had been many, but nothing that'd happened with other boys even began to compare the madness that'd overtaken me when Max's lips touched mine.

But he'd shoved me away and barked at me to go inside. Then he'd disappeared into the night so quickly that I questioned my sanity. Had he been there at all? It seemed surreal now: Max waiting at my door with a bottle of wine; our argument over Niko while I huddled in his jacket; my intense, mindless reaction to his kiss.

I rubbed at the persistent ache in the center of my chest and leaned back on the padded seat of the cab with a sigh. Today had been miserable. This morning, I'd barely gotten through Saturday brunch with my dad without bursting into tears. He'd been able to tell something was wrong with me, and I'd had to lie. I'd babbled about work stress or something. I couldn't quite remember. The entire day had been a blur, and I couldn't wait to get home.

My heart leapt for a moment. What if Max was waiting for me on my front porch?

I wanted to talk to him so badly. And I never wanted to see him again. My emotions were a tangled mess when it came to Max Ferrara.

For the dozenth time today, I yanked my fingers away from my lips. I kept tracing them, struggling to ease the phantom tingle that his kiss seemed to have branded into my flesh.

It was absolutely insane to think that I'd kissed the man who'd kidnapped me and tied me to a chair in his basement. No matter if he'd saved my life when that car had been rushing right at me. No matter if he'd tried to protect me from Niko because of his misguided belief that the Russian was somehow dangerous. No matter if the pain in his eyes when he said he was a monster made my heart tug toward him.

I rubbed my chest again, pressing my palm tight against my sternum to alleviate the ache.

I felt raw, my nerves ragged and painfully exposed. Tonight, I'd barely been able to withstand Gavin's snide remarks at our networking event. It'd taken all my willpower to drag myself to the meeting of the Legal Networking Group, and my bully had made it every bit as miserable as I'd feared. Every time I'd turned around, he'd seemed to be lurking close by, waiting to get in a snide insult or passive aggressive remark. By then end of the night, he'd been visibly inebriated, and he'd become even more persistent in his efforts to rattle me, that nasty smile tainting his otherwise handsome features.

I was rattled enough without Gavin's torment. I had much bigger issues than my childhood bully to cope with.

Some of the tension eased from my muscles when the cab turned onto my street. Almost home. I could hardly wait to cuddle up beneath my fuzzy pink blanket with a book and a glass of pinot.

The memory of the wine Max had brought me

flashed through my mind, drawing a shiver to the surface of my skin. He'd known what kind I liked because he'd broken into my home and rifled through my belongings. That violation still shook me to my core, even if I'd come to understand him better since then.

When I'd stepped outside this morning, the bottle hadn't been where I'd abandoned it on the front step. I wasn't sure if Max had taken it with him or if someone else had cleaned it up. Last night, I'd been too desperate to scramble away from his dark mood to even think about the wine.

He'd seemed furious with me, but he'd been the one to initiate the kiss. And yet, he'd glowered at me as though it'd been my fault.

A spark of anger flickered in my chest, and I stoked it. Anger was a much less messy emotion to cope with than the sickening swirl of hurt and confusion that'd haunted me all day. I had a terrible suspicion that the persistent sting at the corners of my eyes and the tightness in my stomach were symptoms of rejection, and that was the most insane thing of all. I should've been relieved that Max had put a stop to our momentary mutual madness. Instead, I felt slightly queasy.

I shook my head to clear away the conflicting

emotions as the cab pulled up in front of my door. No Max waiting on my front porch.

I resolutely ignored the sinking sensation in my chest, paid the fare, and stepped out onto the sidewalk. I hadn't made it two steps when a second car door slammed a few yards behind me.

"Freckles!"

My stomach dropped to the pavement. *No.* Gavin couldn't be here. He didn't love tormenting me enough to follow me home. That was too far, even for him.

Refusing to glance over my shoulder, I quickly marched to my front door.

"Hey, Freckles! Don't walk away from me."

Oh my god. That was definitely Gavin's alcohol-slurred voice.

My disbelief that he'd pursued me all the way to my house was washed away by a wave of nausea. I had to get inside and lock the door between us.

I'd managed to reach my front stoop when his hand snagged my wrist. "I'm talking to you," he said hotly, demanding my attention.

I rounded on him, releasing all my roiling emotions in a burst of rage. "What the hell are you doing here, Gavin?"

He stepped toward me. I took a step back and bumped against my door. He crowded me, his tall frame dwarfing mine. Fear skittered down my spine, and I tried to yank my hand free from his grip. His fingers tightened, clenching hard enough to leave a bruise. Just like he'd done when we were teenagers. I couldn't smother a wince, and his white teeth flashed in a savage grin.

"You drive me crazy, you know that? I think you do." He leaned in, and the stale scent of beer washed over my face, making my stomach turn. "You like driving me crazy, little tease. I think you wear these tight skirts just for me." His free hand sank into my hip, squeezing harder than his fingers on my wrist.

A humiliating whimper slipped through my pursed lips before I could stifle it. He grinned.

"Fuck, you're so hot."

"Let me go," I seethed, trying to twist away. His hands clamped down harder. Pain shot through my hip and wrist, and I swallowed another shameful sound of distress. I lifted my chin, drawing on my years of practice in dealing with this bully. I barely succeeded in keeping my posture straight. He'd never touched me like this before. He'd never pinned me and looked at me with lust clouding his navy eyes.

Backing down and cowering wasn't an option, no matter how much this new aspect of his cruelty unnerved me. My hand fisted around my keys in my purse. If I had to, I'd use them as a weapon.

But my dad was the mayor. This could cause a scandal. Even if the altercation wasn't my fault, it would end up in the news if I seriously hurt Gavin.

And judging by the harshness of his hold, I'd have to use significant force to get him to release me. He was drunk and probably had eighty pounds on me. I had no idea what he was capable of. I never would've imagined this awful scenario, and his unpredictability was scary as hell.

"I've let you get away with harassing me at the office because I didn't want to cause any professional tension." Only years of practice allowed me to keep my voice calm and even. "But if you don't let me go right now, I'll file criminal charges."

I tried to jerk away again, but his fingers dug in deeper as his handsome features twisted into a scowl. "You think you're too good for me, but I bet you're a dirty little slut now that you're all grown up. The ugly ones always turn into desperate sluts. You're lucky I even want to fuck you."

My hand firmed around my keys, and I slid the sharpest one between my fingers, ready to gouge him. I'd never hurt anyone before, and my stomach turned at the prospect of drawing blood.

He released my hip, and I sucked in a shuddering

breath. He was going to back off. I wouldn't have to strike him.

Then, his hand roved lower, dipping behind me to grope my butt.

Panic spiked, and my composed mask shattered. "Stop!" I shrieked, completely losing my calm façade. "Let me go!"

Acting on blind instinct, I wrenched my keys out of my purse and swung. Before the sharp metal could connect with his face, a terrible snarl ripped through the air, and Gavin's pawing hands were jerked away from my body. He fell back, his arms flailing for balance. A familiar dark shadow shoved my assailant farther away from me. Gavin tripped down the stairs and hit the pavement with a bone-shattering *crack.*

Max was on him before the ragged cry finished leaving his chest. My protector's meaty fist slammed into Gavin's jaw, and his head snapped to the side. He drew his fist back again, pummeling the man who'd groped me.

A sharp exclamation to my right tore my horrified focus away from the two men. A middle-aged couple had stopped on the sidewalk several yards away. The man's arm clasped the woman tight to his side, edging his body between hers and the violence unfolding at my feet. Her hand was clapped over her chest, and her eyes were wide. "Call the police!" she urged her partner.

A thrill of alarm shuddered through me. The cops couldn't come here. They'd arrest Max for assault. And he'd be implicated in a police report with my name in it. If I wanted to keep him off my dad's radar, I couldn't allow that to happen.

"Max!" I cried, turning my attention back to the grappling men. Gavin was sprawled beneath him, blood splattering the pavement and dripping from his split lips. "Max, stop!"

My dark protector went rigid, freezing with his fist pulled back in midair. I hurried toward them and clasped his shoulder before he could change his mind. Powerful muscles rippled and flexed beneath my touch, but he didn't take his eyes off my attacker.

Gavin's eyes were wild, his bloody lips slack with horror. Was that terrified expression the same one that'd contorted my features the first time I'd seen Max's scarred, rage-twisted face?

My heart ached, and my hand firmed on his shoulder. "You have to stop," I said gently. "Someone will call the cops."

His fist dropped, but he lowered his snarling face closer to Gavin's. My bully squirmed and tried to scramble away. Max grabbed his shirt, trapping him under his menacing scowl.

"Never touch her again." The words were so gravelly that they were barely discernible, but Gavin nodded with a shaky jerk of his head.

"I won't. I swear. I didn't. Jesus…" He babbled beneath the crushing weight of Max's rage and the terrifying sight of his damaged face, twisted with dark retribution.

Max recoiled from Gavin as though my bully was suddenly toxic. He shoved to his feet, positioning his big body between me and my tormentor. I peeked around his bulky frame, keeping my eyes on the threat even as I huddled behind my protector.

My keys were still in my fist, the metal digging into my palm with the intensity of my grip. Max had spared me from having to gouge Gavin's face. There wasn't so much as a speckle of blood on my hand.

But Max's knuckles were painted red with Gavin's blood. He appeared entirely unharmed, but my bully huddled on the pavement, moaning and clutching his right arm. I remembered the sickening crack when he'd fallen down the stairs, and I wondered if he'd broken bone.

Something savage seared the inside of my chest. I hoped it hurt like hell. Judging by the tears streaming down his face, diluting the crimson blood that dripped from his lips, Gavin was in a lot of pain.

Good. He'd caused me an ocean of pain over the years. He'd followed me home, groped me, and left bruises on my skin. I wasn't sure what else he would've done to me if Max hadn't come to my defense.

"Leave," Max seethed, his chest rising and falling on heavy breaths. He hadn't even broken a sweat, but his entire body practically thrummed with suppressed violence.

Gavin stumbled to his feet, cringing when his arm shifted at the movement. He cradled it to his chest, blinking hard as more tears fell. His navy eyes shifted to me, fear morphing into familiar contempt. "Is this your boyfriend, Freckles?"

Max's body went eerily still. "Don't look at her. Look at me." His voice was a harsh rasp, and I resisted the urge to step away from his palpable menace.

Instead, I edged closer to him, keeping the solid barrier between Gavin and me. My bully could easily harm me, but Max had made it abundantly clear that the spoiled rich boy couldn't hurt him.

"Never come here again." That same gravelly, bone-chilling tone. "Don't talk to her. Don't breathe the same air as her. If you do, I'll know."

Gavin's tanned skin paled, and he swallowed hard before he managed to gather some false bravado. His chin jutted up as he sneered, "And what are you going to do about it, ugly?"

Max remained utterly still, as though his body was carved from ice. From my vantage point, I could only see him in profile, but the cruel grin that split his scarred features made my stomach knot.

"I'll break more of your bones." The threat was a calm statement of fact. "We can start right now if you want. You have three seconds to walk away. She won't be able to stop me next time."

Gavin's face went a sickly shade of green, and his eyes briefly flickered to me. A low warning sound that was purely predatory rumbled from Max, and he shifted to hide me from my bully's view.

Without thinking, I touched my hand to his lower back, as though that would be enough to tether him to me. "Don't," I whispered. My voice was too quiet for Gavin to hear me, but Max's muscles uncoiled ever so slightly beneath my fingertips. He didn't advance on my attacker.

Despite my vindictive pleasure at Gavin's suffering, I really didn't want that older couple to call the cops. They'd crossed the street to avoid the conflict, but they still hovered nearby, monitoring the situation. The man hadn't pulled out his phone, but that didn't mean he'd hesitate to contact the police if violence broke out again.

Gavin's bloody lips twisted with contempt, and he spat at Max's feet before turning and stalking away. Within a few yards, he managed to hail a taxi, retreating from the threats issued by my dark protector.

My hand firmed on Max's back as I leaned into him for support. My knees were suddenly shaky, and my teeth clicked together as my skin pebbled. I hadn't realized that I'd been riding an adrenaline high until the danger passed, and now I felt weirdly tingly and lightheaded.

Max turned to me, his big hands gently grasping my shoulders to steady me. Those black eyes were soft as they roved over each of my features, assessing. His hair was still pushed back from his brow, his scar fully visible. But I didn't experience even a twinge of fear. His terrifying scowl had scared off my assailant. The mark might look frightening, but it couldn't hurt me.

Max wouldn't hurt me.

"Are you okay?" he asked, his voice deep and soothing.

"Y-yeah." The word shook, and I realized I was lying. I wasn't okay. That'd been deeply disturbing, and Gavin's new kind of sexual aggression shook me to my core. "No," I admitted. "Not really."

Max cocked his head at me, those deep, dark eyes

intent on every nuance of my expression. "You should sit down. Eat something. Hydrate." He nodded in the direction of my front door. "Go on."

"I don't have any food in my fridge," I said without thinking. Earlier, I'd been too distracted to go to the store for my weekend grocery run, and I'd been so anxious that I hadn't been hungry, anyway. Now, my stomach twisted with a sudden hunger pang, and my fingers shook.

His full lips pressed together in a thin, disapproving line. "Okay. I'll take you someplace. Where do you like to go around here?"

"Pairings," I replied automatically. It was my favorite local spot, just around the corner from my apartment. They had an epic charcuterie and cheese board. It was my comfort food place where I went to unwind when I wanted to go out with my friends but stay close to home.

Max's brows lifted. "That's a wine bar, right? You need to eat something."

"They have food," I countered, suddenly ravenous. "I can go order takeout. You don't have to come with me."

He wrapped a strong arm around my shoulders and tucked me close to his side. "Well, I am. I'm not leaving you alone until you're safely back in your apartment."

I started walking alongside him, deciding not to argue. I was still shaken by what Gavin had done, and truthfully, I didn't want to be alone right now. I wouldn't feel safe out here, but I really did want to eat something.

"Okay," I agreed, leaning into him slightly as we walked toward my comfort place. I needed the support, even if it came from the most unlikely person imaginable. The man who'd kidnapped and interrogated me only a couple of weeks ago had saved me multiple times. I was safe with him, no matter how scary he looked.

$\mathcal{M}$y hands were still shaking when I sat down on one of the cushy black leather barstools at Pairings. The host recognized me as a regular, and he'd made sure to seat me at one of my favorite high-top tables near the window. I rubbed my palms over my chilled arms. Right now, I would've preferred a table tucked into a safe corner, where I wouldn't have to worry about being watched or followed.

I was worried about Gavin, my bully and now my assailant. The twinge in my hip as I sat served as an awful reminder of his cruel, possessive grip. I shuddered and hugged my arms more tightly around myself.

"He's gone. He won't touch you again." Max's voice was a low growl.

My eyes snapped to his. Despite the rough anger in his tone, his gaze was tight with concern for me. Only one of his dark eyes was fully visible, the other once again concealed by his carefully tousled hair. He'd hidden his scar and tucked away his terrible, enraged mask.

I wouldn't have been scared even if he'd been snarling at me. I was completely safe with Max.

"Thank you," I murmured, finally releasing my aching chest from my own protective embrace.

I reached out and placed my hand over his where it was fisted on the tabletop. Crimson lines had settled into the creases around his knuckles, Gavin's blood clinging to him even after he'd wiped most of it off on his black shirt. When I touched the lingering traces of the violent scene, his jaw firmed, and his fingers flexed. For a moment, I thought he'd pull away.

Then, he blew out a breath and relaxed. He turned his hand and pressed his palm to mine, interlacing our fingers. I felt shockingly small in his grasp, every bit as delicate as he'd said. I'd definitely felt weak when Gavin had me pinned against my front door. Max was even taller and broader than my bully, but his imposing size didn't elicit so much as a tremor of fear. Instead, that strange, honeyed warmth pooled low in my belly, the same unfamiliar sensation that'd overcome me when he'd held me in place for his savage kiss.

My face heated, and his eyes flicked to my pink cheeks. His dark gaze picked each of my features apart once again, focusing on me with an intensity that I'd never experienced before. It made something decidedly feminine quiver inside me. The masculine attention was both gratifying and slightly unnerving. I resisted the urge to shift in my seat to alleviate the odd tingling that'd crept up my thighs.

"You really aren't scared of me." He said it like an impossibility, something that completely defied reality.

My mouth curved in a small smile. "You're finally listening to me, huh? No, I'm not scared of you, Max. And don't tell me I should be." I spoke before he could get the words out. "You can't tell me what to think or feel, so don't waste your breath."

"Stubborn," he muttered, a ghost of an accusation.

"So are you," I countered coolly.

His lips quirked. "I'm glad you're feeling better. You seem to love arguing with me."

I scoffed. "Only because you say ridiculous things."

He laughed, a strangely raspy sound, as though his vocal cords weren't used to it. His mouth tilted in a crooked grin, and his eyes sparkled. My breath caught in my throat. Max was beautiful. I'd seen glimpses of it before, but his smile was stunning enough to knock me square in the chest.

Before I could snap my slack jaw closed, our server appeared. "Pinot noir and a charcuterie, Allie?" he asked, recognizing me.

I nodded in rote agreement, unable to tear my eyes from Max's handsome face. His features firmed to something stern, but not scary. The slight press of his full lips and warning slant of his dark brow made my stomach do a funny flip.

"And a water," he said firmly, adding to my order. His gaze flicked to our server. "I'll have the same as her."

"Thanks," I mumbled in the man's direction as he hurried off to the bar. I couldn't seem to look away from Max. I'd only ever seen him in shadow, where darkness pooled beneath the sharp lines of his face. There was nothing frightening about his appearance now. The warm lighting in the intimate, wood-paneled bar illuminated his golden skin and danced over his obsidian eyes. He looked like a fallen angel.

Suddenly, looking directly at him was almost unbearable. Flames licked my veins, and my skin flushed hot enough to make me blush from my ears all the way down to my chest.

"I think your freckles are cute," he said abruptly, his voice a deep rumble.

My eyes snapped to his, and my brain scrambled to catch up. "What?"

"Before. When I called you Freckles." I flinched at the nickname, and he frowned. "I said it because I think they're cute. I didn't know it was upsetting for you."

I pressed my lips together, holding in the retort that being tied up in his basement had been upsetting. Caustic words would make him retreat behind that angry mask that obscured his pain, and I didn't want to lose him. Despite how we'd met, I craved more time with my dark protector, the damaged man who defended me so fiercely.

The man who'd kissed me with such passion that my lips still tingled with the memory of his mouth on mine.

Was that why he'd been outside my place tonight, close enough to protect me from Gavin's sick advances? An insane part of me had craved to see him again, to find him waiting for me on my front porch. Did he feel the same way about our kiss? Hot and confused and greedy for more?

"Why were you outside my place tonight?" I asked, peeking up at him through my lashes. I was suddenly anxious for his answer, and my insides coiled tight in the few seconds it took him to respond.

"Because I couldn't stop thinking about you," he finally admitted, his voice an intimate rumble that rolled through my body like deep thunder in a warm summer storm.

"I was thinking about you too." Was that my breathy whisper? He leaned into me, and I swayed toward him. The table separated us, but I could feel his body heat pulsing against mine.

I jolted when the server clicked down our wine glasses. Embarrassment seared my cheeks. I'd totally forgotten we were in public.

Before I could pull away, Max's hand tightened on mine, holding me captive. His strong fingers were iron bands, holding me in a careful but unbreakable cage. I relaxed in his grip. I didn't want him to let me go.

The server set down a huge wooden platter featuring a mouthwatering spread of my favorite cured meats and aged cheeses. My stomach rumbled with a painful ache, reminding me of my intense hunger. Keeping one hand in Max's, I reached out and plucked up a slice of Iberico ham to alleviate my sudden ravenousness. I moaned at the rich, decadent flavor. God, my fancy comfort food had never tasted so good.

Max's nostrils flared, and his eyes sparked, keen on every nuance of my rapturous expression.

I squirmed beneath his scrutiny, a little embarrassed at my enthusiastic response. I would've made that little sound of delight in front of my friends, but Max was looking at me like I'd just moaned into his mouth while he was kissing me. The memory of the wanton, animal sounds we'd made as we exchanged ragged breaths played through my mind, and that molten honey sensation slid down my spine.

I was too hot and weirdly tingly. I took a gulp of my wine to calm my jittery nerves.

"Water," Max said, that stern, masculine tone stoking the heat inside me. "You need to hydrate, not get drunk."

"I won't get drunk," I replied defensively. Was I pouting? I hastily reached for my water and gulped that instead.

"Good." His deep, satisfied tone caressed my skin like an intimate touch. The achy pulse between my legs that I'd experienced for the first time when he'd kissed me started to thrum once again.

I drank more water to cool down. It didn't help.

"Don't you want to eat some?" My voice was strangely high pitched as I gestured at the spread, trying to distract myself with some normal conversation.

He tipped his head at the platter. "You finish what you want first. This isn't exactly a meal." A small frown creased his brow.

"And what would you prefer?" I countered, still slightly defensive. Max had me totally off balance.

"I'd prefer if you ate something more substantial. You're rattled after what that asshole tried to do to you." His frown twisted into his most fearsome scowl.

I squeezed his hand, drawn to comfort him rather than fear him. "Thank you for pulling him off me. I don't know what he would've done if you hadn't been there."

Max's scowl remained fixed in place, but it wasn't directed at me. "If I'd realized he was a threat to you, I would've punched him sooner. I thought you might be together when he first showed up. Then you shouted at him to let you go." His eyes flashed. "I never should've let him touch you."

His gaze remained dark and distant, and his hold on my hand shifted so that his fingertips brushed over my wrist. I followed the direction of his glower and saw that my skin was red where Gavin had grabbed me. Max traced the tender spot, the light rasp of his callouses making my flesh tingle.

"How do you know that bastard?" he growled.

"I've known Gavin since high school," I replied

with a sigh, spilling out my pain without hesitation. I didn't experience even a flicker of worry that Max would use the knowledge of my vulnerability against me. "He was a bully then, and he's a bully now. We work at the same internship, and I have to see him almost every day. We had a networking event tonight, and I guess he got his cab to follow mine home." The tingling sensation on my wrist intensified, making me hyperaware of Max's touch. "He's never done anything like that before."

Max's jaw ticked, but his fingers remained gentle on my skin. "I'm sorry I called you Freckles," he said tightly. "I heard that fucker call you that. I'm not a bully, and I didn't say it to be cruel."

"I know." My skin pebbled, and I wasn't sure if it was in response to his intimate touch or because we were both remembering that awful night in his basement. I'd called Max a bully then. He seemed to have made the connection to Gavin's history of cruelty.

"Eat," he prompted.

Obediently, I popped a slice of aged Manchego cheese into my mouth. The buttery, nutty flavor had never tasted so decadent. I really was hungry, and all of my senses were oddly heightened. I wasn't sure if it was a result of the adrenaline dump or because everything seemed to sparkle when Max was touching me.

"You should try some," I urged, struck with the desire to share something I loved with him. I wanted to see him smile again. "It's really good."

He eyed the spread dubiously. "I'll pass."

"Oh, come on." I rolled my eyes at him. "It's delicious and decadent, and it makes you feel fancy. I love a charcuterie."

His lips twitched with amusement. "What if I don't like being fancy? What if I want a cheeseburger and dirty fries?"

"Then you should've suggested a diner," I said flippantly.

"Next time." He said it like a warning, but I thrilled at the dark promise.

Next time? He wanted to do this again? Wait, were we on a date right now?

I watched him sample some Roquefort, grimace, and take a gulp of pinot to wash away the blue cheese flavor. A giggle bubbled from my chest. He set the wine glass down, his full attention fixing on me in that way that made my belly quiver.

"This tastes awful, Bambi."

I rolled my eyes and selected a Marcona almond before nudging the salty snack in his direction. "You've barely tried it. Just avoid the blue cheese. And don't call me Bambi."

He shot me a crooked smile, and I forgot how to

breathe. "But you get all flushed and cute when I call you Bambi. You don't really mind it, do you?" He brushed his calloused fingertips over the sensitive skin at the inside of my wrist, feeling my pulse speed up in response to his teasing.

My cheeks flamed, and his grin turned dazzling.

"Eat your almonds," I muttered, hot and flustered.

He laughed, and it didn't sound so raspy this time. He sampled an almond, grunted in approval, and ate another.

"See?" I said, a silly grin stretching my lips. "You should try more. Trust me."

He gave me a sardonic nod. "Okay, Bambi. I trust you."

He started picking at different options on the platter, less hesitant with each bite. I began explaining what each item was and where it originated. He listened with rapt attention, as though my inane babbling about my favorite food was the most fascinating thing he'd ever heard. By the time the spread had almost disappeared and our wine glasses were empty, I felt pleasantly warm, and a light buzz tingled over my head.

"Feeling better?" he asked, his massive body fully relaxed and his sharp features content in a way I never would've imagined even an hour ago. He hadn't once let go of my hand since we'd arrived at the bar.

"Yes, much better. Thank you." I gave his fingers a little squeeze to convey my gratitude. He'd helped me relax too. After that awful ordeal with Gavin, he'd managed to put me completely at ease.

He squeezed back. "Let's get you home."

We asked for the check, and he insisted on paying. Was this really a date? It felt like a date.

But he hadn't asked me out. In fact, he'd kind of commanded me to go and eat something, and he'd informed me that he would be joining me. That didn't exactly sound like a date.

He tucked me under his arm as he walked me home, and I nestled into his warmth. He smelled like leather and man. The tingling in my head zinged along my veins, spreading all the way to my fingers and toes.

We reached my front door, and he started to pull away. I turned into him, unwilling to let him go. My lips felt swollen and achy from his ferocious kiss, and I wanted more.

Moving with a swiftness that shocked us both, I twined my arms around his muscular shoulders and pushed up onto my toes. He met me halfway, and our mouths collided in a rush of heat and raw need. I didn't challenge him this time. I didn't want to clash my will against his. My head tipped back, welcoming him to claim me.

His low groan rumbled over my tongue and down into my core. That aching throb between my legs tempted and tormented me, and I molded my body to his.

He took a step toward me, backing me up until I bumped into the door. His massive body surrounded me, pinning me in place for his devastating kiss. His big hand wrapped around my hip, branding my flesh with masculine heat. The slight twinge of pain beneath his grip reminded me that this was exactly where Gavin had grabbed me.

I whimpered into his mouth, and his lips softened, coaxing me to relax. He handled me gently, careful not to bruise, but he resolutely held my hip exactly where my bully had hurt me. There was something possessive and utterly primal about his touch, and the heat of his hand burned away the lingering taint left by Gavin's groping fingers.

I melted against him, inviting him to deepen our kiss. His mouth firmed on mine, claiming me with renewed ferocity in response to my surrender. The wild hunger we shared overwhelmed us both, and my hands shaped around his bulging muscles as he pressed closer, pinning me in place for his demanding kiss.

Finally, he pulled back just enough to allow us both to gasp for air. He kept one hand firmly on my hip, maintaining his possessive but gentle grip. His other forearm braced against my front door beside my head, caging me in as we exchanged ragged breaths. Unlike our last kiss, he didn't rest his forehead on mine. This close, I could see that every fine line around his left eye was drawn with strain, as though he was holding himself back.

I didn't care about his scar touching my brow, but it seemed he wasn't ready for that kind of contact. It was somehow more intimate than his mouth on mine. The inch of space between our faces was suddenly a solid barrier, a wall that protected his worst vulnerability.

I wanted to show him that his scar didn't matter to me. I'd been bullied for my appearance for most of my life, and I'd watched his awful sister inflict cruel emotional wounds while Max remained silent, allowing her to lash him. All I cared about was the feel of his sensual lips caressing mine, his intoxicating scent, and his protective instincts. I'd never burned this hot for any man, and I wanted more.

I went up on my toes, seeking another kiss. His hand left my tender hip to grasp my waist, pushing me back against the door. He kept that invisible barrier between us, but he swayed toward me even as he denied us both.

"If we don't stop now, I'll do something you might regret." His warning rumbled over my sensitized lips.

"I don't regret kissing you." My voice was breathy and sultry in a way that was entirely unfamiliar to me. I tried to close the distance between us again, but he pinned me firmly in place, restraining me with an unbreakable hold.

"Allie…" He groaned my name, as though it caused him physical pain to hold himself back. "I want you. I want you so fucking bad. You don't know what you do to me."

His square jaw was tight, his sharp features drawn with feral hunger.

"Then kiss me again," I whispered. The pulsing between my legs intensified, tugging me toward him.

He refused to close the distance between us, even though his eyes sparked with something like pain. "If I kiss you again, I won't stop. I'll push you up against this door and explore every inch of your hot little body. I won't give a fuck who can see us. If you don't want witnesses when I claim you, we'll have to take this inside."

For a moment, the memory of his hands restraining me in a different way flashed across my mind: he'd clamped his big hand over my mouth, pinned me to the wall in my foyer, and slid a needle into my neck.

I stiffened in his arms, and his mouth twisted in a grimace, as though he tasted something rotten.

"That's what I thought," he said bitterly.

Abruptly, he stepped back. Cool air slapped my skin where his warm body had touched mine. A soft gasp left my lips, my chest tightening. Without thinking, I grabbed his wrist.

"Wait." My voice took on a ragged, pleading edge. I couldn't bear his pain, his distance. I wanted him to lose himself in me, just like I lost myself in him whenever he was near.

He went utterly still, his chin lifted in a challenging sneer. But he didn't pull his hand free from my desperate grip.

"This was a mistake." He bit out each word. "I won't bother you again."

"No!" I refused, my fingers tightening around his wrist.

His brow drew low over his left eye, the scarred side of his face completely obscured in the shadow of his dark curls. "You want me to keep stalking you?" He delivered a derisive challenge, his lips still twisted in that cruel sneer.

I'd hit a nerve, and he was pushing me away to

protect himself. I wondered if he'd let anyone this close to him since his accident. His sister had taunted that I'd been the first person to date him. How long had he been bereft of touch? Of affection?

My heart squeezed. I wasn't ready to let him inside my home. I wouldn't be able to smother my lingering trauma from that horrific night, and it would sour our connection. Whatever wild, hungry thing we shared was new and fragile, and I liked it too much to see it destroyed.

I didn't want to see *him* destroyed. And the reflexive physical signs of my remembered terror shredded him.

I am a monster out of your worst nightmares. He hadn't behaved monstrously since that night. I suspected his desperate actions went against his true nature. And the reminder of the awful thing he'd done to me made him slip behind that frightening mask, another barrier between us.

I wouldn't let him do it. He'd protected me, even when I protested. When I was with him, I didn't have to pretend to be strong all the time. I didn't have to fight through my anxiety to prove to people that I was capable and independent. Max had seen me at my most vulnerable after Gavin's attack, and he hadn't judged me for being weak and shaken. He'd insisted on helping me calm down.

He'd helped me reclaim my own strength by supporting me through the worst of the traumatic experience.

I wanted for him to be vulnerable with me, too. I was safe with Max, but he was safe with me. He had to know that.

"No, I don't want you to stalk me," I replied, keeping my tone low and calm. "I want to give you my number."

His jaw ticked. "That's a bad idea, Bambi."

Oh. We were back to nicknames now.

Well, I wouldn't let him put that kind of distance between us. I no longer hated being called Bambi, but this moment was too important to allow him to retreat from me. If I let him walk away now, I might never see him again. He would bury himself in his rage. He would keep pursuing his vendetta against my father, and he'd probably end up in prison, further suffering for a family that'd deceived him.

Love his hard, but blood is everything. His haunting declaration ghosted through my mind.

Love shouldn't be hard, and Max didn't deserve any more pain than he'd already endured.

"You don't get to tell me what to do and how to feel, remember?" I reminded him gently. "I want to see you again."

"You really are crazy." I suspected that the words

were meant as a blow, but the longing that roughened his tone betrayed the depth of his desire.

My free hand twitched toward him, drawn to comfort him. But I sensed that he'd back away farther if I dared to make tender contact. He was feeling too vulnerable, and his default was to bury any signs of perceived weakness, hiding them even from himself.

I fixed him with a level stare instead and held out my hand between us, palm-up. "Give me your phone."

He remained motionless for a long moment, glowering down at me. I didn't flinch or cower. I simply waited for him to surrender.

You don't scare me.

"Max," I prompted.

His name on my lips seemed to be a trigger for him, and he reached into his pocket to retrieve his phone even as he continued to scowl at me.

I lifted my brows and waited, expectant.

Nope. Still not scared.

He blew out a long sigh and typed in his passcode, unlocking the phone before handing it to me. I accepted it and quickly entered my contact details before he could change his mind and snatch it back. I fired off a text to myself so that I'd have his number, too.

"There," I said, satisfied. I returned his phone. "Now you don't have to stalk me anymore."

"I have been stalking you. It's not a joke." He said it like a dark reminder, as though I'd somehow forgotten his madness and the terrible way we'd first met.

"You also saved me from getting hit by a car and protected me from Gavin," I countered. "I'd prefer to be able to ask you to meet up than to find you lurking in the shadows." My lips twitched, teasing.

"That's not funny," he half-growled, still trying to scare me off.

I lifted my chin and met him head-on. "I want to see you again," I said firmly. "I'll text you."

He shook his head at me. "You shouldn't."

"That's really annoying, you know," I informed him flippantly. "Stop telling me what I should and shouldn't do."

His mouth quirked at the corners, as though he was suppressing a smile of his own. "I think you're infuriating, too."

I rolled my eyes at him. White flames danced over his dark, intent gaze. They licked my skin, and my body began to tingle with the memory of his wicked kiss. My tongue darted out to wet my lips, craving more. His eyes riveted to my mouth, and he swayed toward me for an instant before his massive frame hardened to granite once again.

"Go inside, Allie." His desire-roughened voice caressed my name, even as he commanded me to leave him.

Moving too quickly for him to stop me, I bounced up onto my toes and brushed a kiss over his cheek. "Goodnight, Max."

A small shudder rolled through him as his bulky muscles flexed, but he restrained himself from crushing me to him for another scorching kiss.

I hesitated for a moment, tempted to test his resolve. I wanted this strong man to come undone beneath my tender hands. The idea made desire pulse deep inside me, and it took effort to force myself to back away.

I still wasn't ready to let him inside, no matter how badly I wanted him. I couldn't bear to taint our connection with echoes of the fear I'd experienced on the night he'd kidnapped me.

Instead of twining my arms around his neck and pulling him close, I turned to unlock my door. He waited in silence, his full focus intent on me as he watched me enter my apartment, guarding me from anyone who might threaten me.

Once I crossed the threshold, I offered Max one final, grateful smile. "I'll see you soon."

It was a firm promise. I wouldn't allow him to retreat from me. I wouldn't allow him to sever the intense, wild connection we shared. And judging by the feral hunger that gleamed in his dark eyes as I shut the door, he wouldn't be able to resist my demands to see him again.

Max burned for me just as hotly as I burned for him.

our escort has arrived. Isabel's text was accompanied by a photo of Davis and Charlie, who were grinning and waving for me to join them.

My heart squeezed. My friends really were the best. When I'd messaged them to blow off some steam about Gavin, they'd all rallied and rearranged their schedules to meet me after work.

My phone vibrated with another text as I stepped onto the elevator that would take me down to the ground floor to meet them.

Davis says to invite Captain Douchebag. We dare him to show his face.

I released a sigh when the elevator doors closed, locking a barrier between me and my tormentor. Gavin had been especially unnerving today. He'd shown up to work wearing a cast and a sling—it turned out he had broken his elbow when he'd hit the pavement. His face was bruised from Max's brutal punches, and I'd overheard him telling a senior colleague that he'd been mugged.

As though the bastard hadn't been the one to commit a crime against *me*.

I didn't breathe a word about what'd really happened. I didn't want to draw any attention to Max.

Gavin hadn't spoken a single cruel word to me all day, but his eyes burned with a new level of loathing I'd never seen before. His hateful gaze seemed to follow me everywhere I went, singeing my skin. His terrible glower promised retribution, and I was worried he might try to accost me again if he followed me home from work.

My besties had come to my rescue. They didn't know anything about Gavin's assault or Max's involvement. They didn't know about Max at all.

But I'd told them Gavin was making me anxious and uncomfortable, and that'd been enough to trigger their protective instincts. They would walk with me to our favorite nearby restaurant, and we would all have a martini and a decadent meal to unwind.

I exited the building and stepped into the flurry

of supportive hugs from my besties. Immediately, the warmth of their love enveloped me, and I squeezed them back. Isabel slung a slender arm over my shoulder and tugged me close as she led me the short distance to the restaurant. Davis practically bounced at our side like a boxer preparing for a fight, issuing dark threats about what he would do to Gavin if I'd let him. Charlie whooped her agreement, my usually mellow friend growing fierce in my defense.

We were just outside the restaurant when my phone rang. For a moment, my heart leapt. What if Max had decided to call me?

I checked the contact details, and my small bloom of joy wilted. I didn't recognize the number.

I held up one finger to my friends, indicating that I needed a minute to answer, just in case it was important or work-related.

"This is Allie Fitzgerald," I answered in my most professional tone.

"Allie." A deep, masculine voice said my name with shocking intimacy. This wasn't a work call. "It's Niko."

My brain stalled out. Niko? As in…

"Nikolai Ivanov," he clarified when I said nothing in response. "We met at your dad's fundraiser on Saturday."

"Oh. Yeah. Hi." I clapped a hand to my forehead. Could I have sounded more awkward?

The last time I'd seen Niko, the impossibly gorgeous man had draped his deliciously man-scented jacket over my shoulders and asked me on a date. Just before Max had stormed out of the darkness and shoved him away.

"I got your number from your dad. I hope you don't mind."

"Oh." My mind scrambled to catch up. Nikolai Ivanov was the last person I'd expected to hear from. I'd barely even thought about him since Max had gotten between us and snarled at him to leave me alone. "I don't mind," I said, automatically polite.

"Good." I could practically hear his dazzling smile over the phone. "Because you never did give me an answer. Can I take you out to dinner sometime? It's the least I can do. I'm pretty sure my dad planted that article. Sorry about that."

"What article?" I could scarcely keep up. The very fact that Niko had called me was baffling. What he was saying made even less sense.

"In the *Times*. I guess you haven't seen it yet." He sighed. "My father isn't very subtle. He definitely approves of you, and he wants to fix us up. Just one date. That's all I'm asking for. If nothing else, it'll get him off our backs. But don't get me wrong," he continued, filling my stunned silence. "I would've asked you out anyway. I'm sorry if he's made things uncomfortable. I hope that doesn't put you off, because I'd really like to see you again."

"But you barely know me." And why had that protest popped out of my mouth? I should be thrilled that a man as devastatingly handsome as Niko was interested in me.

"I'd like to get to know you," he countered smoothly. "Are you free this Saturday?"

"Oh, um. Sure." I was so flustered that my agreeable nature overwhelmed reason. This was far too jarring, and he'd caught me completely off guard.

And what was this whole article-thing about?

"Great. I'll text you, and we can work out the details."

"Okay," I agreed, my mouth moving on autopilot.

He ended the call, and I stared at my phone for a second, stunned.

"Who was that?" Davis asked. "You look totally shook. Was it that douchebag?"

"No." I blinked, trying to clear my head in the wake of the short, dizzying phone call. "It was Nikolai Ivanov. He asked me out."

"Oh my god!" Isabel squealed. "Hot, billionaire heir Nikolai Ivanov? From the fundraiser?"

"Yeah."

"Wait, I saw him talking to you," Charlie chimed in. "He's totally gorgeous. Why do you look sick? Don't you want to go out with him?"

"No." My refusal was firm and immediate, and for some reason, Max's dark eyes flashed through my mind. "I mean, I don't know. He said something about an article his dad planted in the *Times*. I got flustered and agreed to a date."

"What article?" Davis already had his phone out, entering my and Niko's names into search. "Ohmygod," he said in a single exhalation. "Holy shit."

"What is it?" Isabel demanded.

We all crowded around the small screen. My stomach dropped when I saw the picture of Niko and me at the fundraiser. His hand was on my arm, and I was staring up at him with a stupidly awed expression on my face. I saw the headline, and I wanted to sink into the pavement: *New York's Own Royal Romance?*

Davis eyed me, a teasing smirk tilting his lips. "All hail Princess Allie!" He offered me a small bow. "Why didn't you tell us you're a royal?"

Charlie slapped his arm. "Read the vibe, Davis. Don't tease her right now." Her big blue eyes were wide with concern. "You okay?"

Isabel snatched the phone from Davis and hastily began reading the article. "I'll give you the

Cliff's Notes," she promised. "Let's get you a martini."

"No," I countered, even as they ushered me forward. "I'd so much rather hear about your audition. And Davis, you had one today too, right? I haven't checked in with you guys since you gave your performances. We don't need to talk about me."

Isabel waved me off. "You're white as a ghost. I know you'll worry about this all night if we don't deal with it right now."

I'd so much rather erase the article's existence from my mind. I turned to Charlie, desperation touching my voice. "Seriously, we've talked about me way too much lately. What about your internship with *Vogue*? I'm so proud of you for landing that, and I feel like we barely discuss it. You must be just as stressed by work as I am."

Charlie shot me a sympathetic smile and shook her head. "Uh-uh. We are so talking about you for a little bit. This is too important to ignore."

Isabel shushed me imperiously. "Hush and let me read. I'll share the deets in just a few minutes."

Somehow, my feet moved, and we were inside the restaurant. My friends urged me into our corner booth, and I dropped down onto the padded leather seat, finally allowing my shaky knees to give out.

I hated the public scrutiny that came along with

being Ron Fitzgerald's daughter. In the past, the press had mostly left me alone other than snapping photos with my dad at important events. It was bad enough that some of the most awkward years of my life were forever memorialized on the internet. Now, that mortifying image of me stupidly staring at Niko would be popping up on thousands of news alerts on people's phones. Anyone who followed the social column of the *Times* would receive a notification, and even a passing glance would ensure that they saw the embarrassing photo.

And oh my god, the royalty thing. Gavin would make my life hell.

"So basically, it's nothing," Isabel declared, returning Davis' phone before pushing my freshly-delivered martini toward me. "Just a fluff piece. It'll fall into obscurity in no time."

"But what does it say?" Davis prompted, leaning forward and resting his chin on his palm, intent on getting more info.

"It just comments on what Allie was wearing—totally complimentary, by the way," she hastened to clarify. "And says how good she and Nikolai look together. It's total clickbait. News about the British royals is really hot right now, so they're just trying to drive traffic based on that. Seriously, it's only speculating that you and Nikolai *might* be dating. There's no substance."

"See, it's not bad at all." Charlie laid a comforting hand on my forearm. "You looked gorgeous in that gown. The photographer saw you sparkling and wanted to get a good shot. I know you don't like the attention, but it's a nice article."

"But I'm not dating Niko," I protested, running a hand through my hair. "And I look so stupid in that picture, ugh."

"Honey, it sounds like you are going on a date with him," Davis said carefully. "Didn't you just agree to go out with him?"

I groaned and reached for my martini, taking a big gulp. The sudden rush of alcohol burned slightly, but I welcomed the small discomfort. Anything to make this awful moment disappear from my brain forever.

"It's okay," Charlie said. "He caught you by surprise. You can cancel the date."

"But…" Isabel hesitated, eyeing me cautiously. "Are you sure you want to? He's gorgeous, Allie. You deserve to have some fun. I know your dad basically scared off any guy who dared to approach you for your entire adult life. Why not go out with a handsome billionaire?"

I shook my head. "Because I like someone else."

The words left my mouth before I fully considered them.

"Okay, wait." Davis held up a hand and glanced at Isabel and Charlie. "Who knew about this?"

My girlfriends shrugged, their full attention fixing on me.

"You like someone?" Isabel leaned toward me, intent on learning every detail. "Who? And why didn't you tell us?"

My cheeks flamed, and I took another gulp of my martini. How the hell could I tell them about Max?

So, this guy kidnapped me and interrogated me in his basement. Then, he stalked me for a while. He wants to blackmail my dad. I've kissed him twice, and I can't stop thinking about him.

Yeah, that would not go over well. I sounded crazy just thinking it to myself.

Charlie plucked the martini glass from my fingers and pulled it a few inches away from me. "Slow down there. You don't have to tell us if you don't want to."

"Yes, she does!" Davis said indignantly. "Spill, Allie."

Mentally, I pushed aside all the reasons I shouldn't like Max and focused on why I'd developed such strong feelings for him. If I thought about it, I'd started softening toward him that night he saved me for the first time.

I blew out a sigh. "Okay, don't freak out, but a few weeks ago I was walking home after our cantina night. I was a little buzzed and didn't pay enough attention to traffic when I was crossing the street. My ankle turned, and I fell. This man, Max, jumped in front of an oncoming car to pull me out of the road."

"You almost got hit by a car, and you didn't tell us?" Isabel's voice was several octaves higher than usual. "That was almost three weeks ago."

"Have you been dating this knight in shining armor for three weeks?" Davis demanded. "Why wouldn't you share this with us? It sounds super romantic."

Charlie's brows rose. "You mean, other than the part where our best friend almost got flattened?"

Davis waved her off and focused on me. "So, have you been secretly dating him this whole time?"

"No." I would have to gloss over the period of time when I'd spent sleepless nights researching his family's crimes. I also couldn't tell them about my awful encounter with his cruel sister, because that was too bound up in his vendetta. My friends couldn't know anything about Max's insane mission against my dad.

"I met up with him again after the fundraiser." I skipped the part where he'd threatened Niko. That would be far too difficult to explain away. "We kissed."

Charlie gasped, Isabel cheered, and Davis gave me a high-five. Sheepishly, I slapped my hand against his.

"But that was just a couple days ago," Isabel pointed out. "It must have been some kiss if you like him enough to blow off Nikolai. It's not like he's your boyfriend, right?"

My stomach flipped at the word. No, Max wasn't my boyfriend. He was... I didn't really have a word for the wild, intense connection we shared.

"I saw him again last night." I paused, debating telling them about Gavin. After a moment, I decided that it was safe to share that particular piece of information. Max's protectiveness had intensified my forbidden feelings for him. If I was going to tell my friends about him, they should know what he'd done for me.

"Max came to my place to pick me up after I got home from my networking event." I fudged the truth just a little. "But Gavin followed me home and..." A chill raced through me at the memory of his groping hands on my body. "Well, it turns out you were right, Davis," I mumbled, staring intently at the polished wooden tabletop. "Gavin does want to fuck me."

"What did he do?" Davis seethed. "I swear to god, I will punch that motherfucker right in his smarmy face."

I swallowed hard and shook my head. "There's no need. Max already punched him in the face. And broke his arm when he pulled Gavin off me."

"I like this guy," Isabel declared. "Why didn't you tell us about him before? He sounds great."

"He's…" I took a moment to search for the right word. "Shy." Well, that wasn't the right word at all, but it would have to do. "He has this burn scar on his face. I get the feeling he doesn't talk to many people because he's self-conscious about it."

Because his cruel sister called him ugly and made him feel like a monster.

My heart twisted just thinking about how terribly she must've treated him since the accident.

"Well, we want to meet him," Charlie said firmly. "He does sound like a decent guy, but we need to vet him."

I blew out a sigh. "I don't think that's a good idea." I could only imagine how Max would react to being grilled by my best friends. He'd probably feel judged and threatened, and he'd retreat behind his wall of rage to protect himself.

"Why not?" Davis demanded.

"Whatever this thing is between us is new," I explained. "And like I said, I don't think he's used to talking to people. If he hadn't saved me from getting hit by that car, I don't think he would've approached me at all."

I realized that much was true. He'd been watching me that night to make sure I didn't go to the cops, but if I hadn't recklessly confronted him, he probably would've disappeared from my life. Our relationship so far had been tumultuous to say the least, but I didn't want to lose what we had.

"Is the scar that bad?" Isabel asked, her voice soft with sympathy. "He really doesn't want to talk to people because of it?"

I nodded. "I'm not sure how or when he got it, but he tries to hide it as much as possible. Whatever happened must've been excruciating and traumatic. I wish he'd realize that I don't care about it. I'm really attracted to him." That was the understatement of the century. Our chemistry was combustible.

"Okay, honey. We'll give you time," Davis allowed. "But we want to meet him."

"We approve of anyone who punches Gavin in the face," Isabel announced.

"Definitely," Charlie added.

I smiled and finally relaxed. My friends' support

meant everything to me, and I was glad I'd been able to tell them about Max. At least, the best parts of Max. The darker things that'd happened between us would never be fully erased, but I chose to focus on the good.

I pulled out my phone and sent him a message: *Meet me at my place in 2 hours?*

A notification popped up telling me that he'd read it almost immediately. But there was no reply. I put my phone away and decided to be present with my friends. Max would either be there when I got home or not. And if he was, this time, I was ready to invite him inside.

CHAPTER 18

MAX

Meet me at my place in 2 hours? I checked the text for the dozenth time, as though it would say something different.

It'd been well over two hours since she'd sent it. Allie was already home. I'd watched to make sure she got inside safely, and no one followed her—not Gavin and not any Russian scum.

I was her only stalker tonight.

My fingers flexed. That was exactly why I had no business accepting her invitation: I was her stalker, not her protector. No matter how much I'd deluded myself, no matter what she'd said, she was still afraid to be alone with me. She was afraid for me to come inside her apartment.

And why wouldn't she be? The last time I'd been inside, I'd drugged and kidnapped her.

My phone buzzed, startling me out of my dark mood.

Another text from Allie: *Are you coming?*

I fired off a response: *You don't want me to come over.*

Three gray dots immediately began bouncing on my screen as she hastily typed her reply: *I asked you to meet me at my place. I wouldn't have asked if I didn't want you to come over.*

I could practically hear that impertinent little huff to her tone as I read the text, and my lips twitched at the corners. I smothered the hint of a smile, forcing myself to remember how she'd shuddered at the prospect of having me in her home. Even on the night I'd saved her from getting hit by that car, she'd been horrified at the idea of me entering her apartment.

I sent her a stark reminder: *It's not safe for you to invite me inside. You don't know what I'm capable of.*

She replied with a challenge: *Then why don't you tell me? What would you do if you were here, Max?*

Heat licked my veins. She was trying to prove a point, but her words unlocked the wicked, forbidden thoughts about her that I'd been obsessing over for weeks.

My fingers flew over the screen before I could think: *I'd pin you against the wall and kiss you until you stop arguing with me. I wouldn't be gentle. I would taste every inch of your hot little body. I would make you moan my name and beg before I finally let you come.*

My breath stuck in my lungs, and I stared at what I'd typed. What I'd already sent in a burst of heated need for her. The message was marked as *read*, but she hadn't replied.

Agonizing seconds passed, and nausea tinged my desire.

Then her reply came through: *Prove it.*

My feet were carrying me toward her door before I could formulate any second thoughts.

CHAPTER 19

ALLIE

Max hadn't been waiting for me when I got home. I'd tried to ignore the way my chest tightened and went about my usual routine to decompress. It was too early to get ready for bed, even if it was a weeknight. I'd changed my professional attire for pajamas before cuddling up on my plush, gray velvet couch. I sank into the mountain of dusky pink pillows and snuggled under my matching blanket as I picked up my latest rom-com. When I opened the book and leafed to the page where I'd left off, the familiar scent of well-loved paper enveloped me just as warmly as my blanket.

For a while, I disconnected from all my problems and disappeared into another world, crafted of beautiful words and sparkling characters. Until Max sent me that insanely hot message, leaving me flushed and flustered in a way only he could.

A knock on my door jolted me, and I clutched the book to my chest, applying pressure to my suddenly racing heart. Gavin's glower filled my mind, and for a second, I froze like a spooked doe.

My phone chimed, sending another little shock through my jittery system. I glanced at the screen. A text from Max: *I'm outside.*

My heartbeat sped up for an entirely different reason. I flung my blanket aside and set down my book on the coffee table, surging to my feet. I paused for a moment, frowning down at the little pink posies that dotted my baby blue silk pajamas.

He knocked again. No time to change. I didn't want him to think fear had gotten the better of me. I still wanted him to come inside.

I rushed to the door, the black and white checked foyer tiles cool against my bare feet. All my senses came alive whenever Max was near, every inch of my body hyperaware of sensation. I didn't fully understand this thrilling connection we shared, but I craved more of it.

I slid back the deadbolt and flung open the door. Max's hulking form was illuminated from the street-lights above, the angle of the light casting shadows beneath the sharp lines of his face. The skull-like mask no longer frightened me. He'd come to see me, but some part of him still wanted to push me away.

His dark eyes glittered as they roved over my body, seeming to trail over each tiny pink flower on my pajamas as he slowly studied me. His gaze followed a lazy path back up to my face, coming to rest on my heated cheeks. The sensual lips that set mine aflame curved into a tilted smirk.

"Cute pjs."

My face burned hotter, mortified that he'd seen me in my childish sleep clothes. I lifted my chin and willed myself to meet his teasing head-on. "You're late. I didn't think you were coming, so I changed into something more comfortable."

"I didn't think I was coming, either. But here I am."

He didn't step inside. He was utterly still, coiled tight with the effort of restraining himself.

My heart squeezed. He didn't realize that I wasn't scared anymore. I wanted to erase this lingering pain between us.

I took a breath and extended my hand, waiting for him to accept it. "I want you to come inside."

His jaw ticked, and the shadows darkened beneath his brow and cheekbones.

I stared up at him, cool and resolute. "That scowl won't work on me," I informed him. "Come in."

His entire body hardened to granite, locking him in place. "I can't take back what I did to you," he rasped. "I told myself I didn't have a choice, but that was a lie. Part of me knew it too. But I took you and terrorized you anyway."

My wrists tingled with the memory of the soft binding that'd secured me to the chair in his basement. I suppressed the urge to rub away the phantom feel of the restraints that had bound me as he'd questioned me.

"I haven't forgotten," I said quietly. "I won't ever be able to forget. But I do forgive you, Max." I reached out and wrapped my fingers around one of his clenched fists. It flexed beneath my touch, his muscles rippling as though resisting an inexorable pull. "I want you to come inside."

Max couldn't resist me any more than I could resist him. If this relationship were at all rational, I'd be screaming for help and locking the door as a barrier between us.

Instead, I gently tugged on his hand, urging him to step over the threshold.

Something snapped inside him, and he surged toward me. His arms wrapped around me, and he captured my shocked gasp with his lips. His strong body pressed forward, entering my personal space as though he had every right. He filled all my senses, his powerful body overwhelming me as the fiery chemistry between us ignited.

I registered the slam of my door as his booted foot kicked it closed behind him. The harsh sound jolted through my body, and I jerked in his arms.

He didn't release me from his savage kiss. Instead, he pushed me back up against the wall, his weight pinning me in place. One of his big hands cupped my nape, his long fingers tangling in my hair and tugging my head back to deepen our kiss.

I quivered in his harsh hold, a thrill of fear dancing through my lust. This wasn't the first time he'd pinned me against this wall and covered my mouth.

But it wasn't his hand smothering my screams this time; his mouth consumed my small whimper, his tongue claiming me in hot, demanding strokes. The kiss was a challenge, a dare.

He craved me as fiercely as I craved him, but some part of him was still trying to push me away, to give me one last chance to escape him.

When my head was spinning and I was trembling in his harsh hold, he finally pulled away to allow me to draw in much-needed oxygen. My knees sagged at the rush, and his strong arms tightened around me, caging me even as he supported me.

"Why aren't you afraid of me?" he growled, his eyes burning with desperate hunger.

His scar was on full display, and for a moment, his twisted snarl made me flash back to the night he'd kidnapped me. My stomach turned when we I realized he'd pinned me in the exact place where he'd drugged me.

He was still trying to scare me off. Well, I wouldn't allow it. My body burned for him, no matter how much he tried to intimidate me.

"Because you're not very frightening." I tried to keep my tone flippant to avoid the deeper feelings of residual terror from overtaking my brain, but my breathy voice hitched slightly. Just because I'd decided that I wanted to be with Max didn't mean that the instinctive part of my mind had forgotten the danger.

I breathed through the echo of fear, and a tantalizing buzz flooded my veins. Maybe my problem wasn't that I couldn't sense the danger Max posed. Maybe I *liked* the danger. I'd never felt more alive than I did when I was in his presence. It was wild and thrilling and possibly a little twisted, but I craved more.

"Allie." Max said my name like a warning, but the

savagery eased from his sharp features. He wrapped his long fingers around my shoulders, holding me with the careful but unbreakable grip that made me feel both sheltered and trapped. A shiver danced over my skin, and I swayed toward him. He frowned down at me.

"Why aren't you afraid of me?" he asked again, more softly this time. His black eyes pinned me in place even more effectively than his strong hands on my shoulders.

He didn't say the next part out loud, but I saw it in the taut lines of his face: *You should be scared.*

He didn't bother to condescend to repeat himself. He'd said it enough times before, and I'd rebuffed him each time, demanding that he respect my autonomy. But he truly didn't understand. I wasn't sure if I fully understood it, either.

"I'm choosing not to be afraid," I replied, my voice still breathless from his merciless kiss. "I know I should be, but I don't want to be. I'm choosing to see you, Max."

The words held so much more weight than implying that I wanted to date him. I s*aw* him: the man beneath the monstrous mask. His pain and protective instincts called to something deep inside me that I couldn't deny.

His mouth descended on mine, hungry for the trust I offered him. His tongue traced my lips, as though savoring the flavor of my fervent words. He kissed me like I was a miracle, his hands bracketing my face with aching gentleness as he claimed me in deep, fierce strokes.

I opened for him, offering him everything he wanted to take.

I trust you. I'm not scared. You're not a monster.

I conveyed each promise with my own fierce kiss, sharing myself with him in a way I'd never connected with anyone else. He'd made himself vulnerable with me, and I willingly put everything on the line for him. I laid my soul bare, and he held me like I was something precious and fragile.

One strong arm wrapped around my waist, tugging me impossibly closer. His other hand left my face to rove lower, long fingers skating down the column of my neck. Just the light brush of his rough callouses on my throat drew a moan from my chest. Fireworks popped and tingled beneath his featherlight touch, my body crackling with awareness.

Suddenly, he cupped my breast, handling me with shocking confidence. I gasped into his mouth, and he hummed his approval, the sound rumbling all the way down to my core. His fingers traced the underside of my breast through my pajamas, and the silky sensation was almost unbearably decadent. My nipples pebbled to hard peaks, and they throbbed gently in time with the deeper ache between my legs.

He brushed his thumb over the tight buds, and hot lines of pleasure sizzled directly from my nipples to my core. Something inside me clenched, and I cried out against his lips.

He groaned, the sound torn between longing and pain. His other hand dipped lower behind my back, his long fingers sinking into my bottom as he clutched me close.

My body molded to his, and he growled into my mouth when my hips rubbed against his hard length.

For a moment, I stiffened. I'd never felt a man's arousal before. It was intimidating and thrilling. A heated rush surged beneath my skin, a wave of feminine gratification.

I did this to him. I made him *want.*

My belly quivered, equal parts aroused and reluctant. As much as I craved Max, I didn't think I was ready to have sex. Just kissing him like this was more than I'd ever experienced with any man.

Suddenly, his grip shifted, and my moment of uncertainty dissipated when the world tilted. One strong arm braced behind my back, and the other hooked beneath my knees. I became weightless as he lifted me up to cradle me against his hard chest.

He held me as though I weighed nothing, and his lips remained hungry and demanding on mine as he carried me to the couch, never once releasing me from his kiss.

He set me down so that I was nestled in the cushions, and he dropped to his knees before me as his hands began to explore my body once again. His mouth lowered, trailing hot kisses over my neck. His hot tongue traced the line of my throat at the same time as his fingers tightened around my nipples.

A ragged cry left my chest, and I arched into him. I wound my arms around his shoulders and pulled him closer, urging him to take more.

He touched me as though he wanted to learn every inch of me, to claim and own. He touched me as though he had every right, and I welcomed his exploration. I had no idea what my body was capable of, and he was wringing pleasure from me in ways I never could've imagined.

His teeth grazed the shell of my ear before he sharply nipped my lobe. The little flare of pain sent an answering pulse of need to my core, and the throbbing between my legs intensified to a deep ache.

A strange, needy sound whined from my chest,

and I writhed in his hands. I didn't know what I wanted him to do. I just needed *more.*

His deft fingers found the delicate buttons at the front of my pajama top, freeing each one with aching slowness. He trailed down my sternum, working his way to my belly, until his hand brushed the spot just above the waistband of my pants.

I gasped and clutched him to me, lifting my hips in silent invitation for more. My fingers tangled in his glossy black curls, and I tried to drag his mouth closer to mine.

It took no effort for him to resist my grasping hands. I felt his slightly cruel smile against my neck, a scrape of his teeth across my vulnerable artery. I whimpered and arched toward him, but he didn't give me an inch.

"You want to come, angel?" The new endearment was hot on my skin as he pressed another gentle kiss to my throat.

One thick finger slid down the hint of exposed flesh between my silky pajama top where he'd undone the buttons without parting the material. He slowly circled my navel and teased just above the waistband of my pants.

I stilled, panting. "I don't..." My cheeks flamed. No man had ever touched me there. My body was on fire. I wanted Max more keenly than I'd known was possible. But I was flustered and more than a little embarrassed at my inexperience.

I wasn't sure when Max had been scarred, but his touch was masterful enough to let me know that he was familiar with a woman's body. He knew exactly how to make me whimper and writhe.

But I didn't know what to do for him. So far, he'd been whipping me into a frenzy, but I'd scarcely done more than welcome his onslaught and clutch him to me.

I bit my lip, and he drew back slightly, his obsidian eyes curious on my face.

"I mean, I've never…" I trailed off, my cheeks burning.

He blinked at me, and his brow furrowed as though he was surprised. "You're a virgin?"

Oh, god. I wanted to sink into the cushions and hide from this mortifying conversation. I was still hot and achy. I wished I hadn't opened my damn mouth.

His eyes roved over my features, reading every nuance of my expression. "It's okay," he soothed. "We don't have to do anything you're not comfortable with, but I am going to make you come. I'm going to make you scream my name." Despite his ferocious expression, he gently grasped my hand and lifted it to his chest, pressing my palm against his heart. It beat rapidly, pumping with his own desire. "I want you, Allie. However you'll have me."

I melted. Max didn't care that I was a virgin. He wouldn't use my inexperience or insecurities to mock me. He looked at me like I was the most beautiful thing he'd ever seen, his sharp features softening with something like awe.

I clasped his nape and surged toward him, crushing my mouth to his. My body ignited on contact, burning and aching for him.

One big hand returned to my breasts, finally parting my top to bare my heated flesh. His calloused fingertips teased and tormented my sensitive nipples, but he didn't move his touch lower. He kept my mouth captive beneath his, feasting on my soft cries and panting breaths as he pinched and played with my breasts, driving me to a frenzy.

I needed release. My skin was too tight, and I could barely contain the pressure that built with every stroke of his tongue against mine. I grasped his hand and directed it toward my waistband. I broke our kiss just long enough to whisper across his lips: "Please. I need you, Max."

His mouth crashed down on mine with a snarl, and he claimed me deeply as his fingers dipped into my silky pajamas. I let out a ragged cry when his fingers brushed over the tight bud between my thighs. I'd never felt so sensitive, like I would explode into a million ecstatic pieces if he allowed me release.

I lifted my hips, silently begging for more. Two fingers rubbed over my lace panties, and the textured material stimulated the most sensitive spot on my body. Electricity crackled through my veins, and I clutched him to me, my hand tugging at his black curls.

He growled into my mouth and applied more pressure, moving his fingers in a tight, circular motion. At the same time, he pinched my nipple hard.

The zing of pain triggered an explosion of plea-sure. Liquid heat rolled through my body in a vicious wave, starting at my core and surging all the way to my fingers and toes. It flooded my mind, sapping me with ecstasy. I screamed his name. He caught it on his tongue, devouring my sounds of pleasure. He continued to stimulate me, wringing more bliss from my body than I'd known was possible.

He toyed with me until I became too sensitive to bear any more. Slowly, he withdrew his hand from my pants and gently cupped my nape, holding me in place as his kiss turned soft and tender.

I shuddered beneath him, the lingering aftershocks of pleasure dancing along my sensitive skin. I breathed him in, allowing myself to sink into everything that was *Max*.

He'd touched me in ways no man ever had, and I didn't want to let him go. I never wanted this to end.

CHAPTER 20

ALLIE

J was cuddled up in Max's lap on my couch, our kisses turning languid. After a long while, he pulled back and allowed us both to catch our breath. His dark eyes roved over my body, studying every inch of me as though it belonged to him.

His calloused fingertips brushed my wrist, and a scowl distorted his features. I followed the direction of his fiery gaze and noted the bruise where Gavin had grabbed me. I'd covered it with a gold cuff bracelet to hide it at the office, but now the mottled purple ring was clearly visible.

"I'm okay," I said softly, even as my stomach turned at the memory of his cruel grip. "My skin just marks up easily."

His black eyes snapped to mine, his white teeth

flashing on a growl. "It's not okay. I should've gotten to you sooner."

I reached out and traced the sharp line of his tight jaw, my fingers tingling at the rough scrape of his stubble. His eyes closed for a moment, and his face relaxed. He leaned into the tender contact.

My heart squeezed. How long had he been denied this simple human touch?

A question about his accident was on the tip of my tongue, but one glance at the brief, serene expression on his face gave me pause. His hair was pushed back, his scar on full display. He seemed to have forgotten to hide it when our bodies were entwined. On some innate level, he was starting to believe he didn't have to hide from me. He was starting to trust me.

I couldn't bear to lose that.

"You did more than enough." I reassured him instead of asking about his scar. "You should've seen Gavin today. He has two black eyes, and his arm is in a cast. He's hurting for what he did to me."

Max's head canted to the side, and his dark gaze picked apart every nuance of my ferocious expression, noting the slightly cruel twist to my lips. "You seem happy that he's in pain."

I shrugged, but my shoulders tensed defensively, and I fiddled with my locket to alleviate the burst of anxiety. Vindictiveness was an ugly quality, but I couldn't bring myself to suppress it. "Am I supposed to feel bad about it?" I challenged.

His features split in a breathtaking, wolfish grin. "No. I like it. He deserved far worse."

I nodded, but I rubbed the smooth back of my locket for comfort. I wasn't sure if I needed soothing because of the implication that I was a vindictive bitch or because I was still rattled by what Gavin had done.

Max's eyes fixed on the necklace. "You don't have to be anxious." He nodded toward where my fingers worried at the warm gold. "I've noticed that you touch it when you're stressed. I've never seen you without it," he explained.

I blinked at him. His perceptiveness should've been slightly unnerving, but his intense focus on my every move made my stomach flip in a decidedly feminine response. Max made me nervous in all the right ways.

"It's all I have left of my mother," I admitted, sharing the information without thought. Max would never use it to hurt me. He'd protected me so many times. I could trust him.

"We lost everything in the fire," I murmured. "I was wearing this when my dad carried me out of the burning house. It was my grandmother's—her name was Alexandra, too. My mom was very close with her, and she wanted me to know that we shared the same tight bond. She gave it to me when I turned ten." The picture of my mother and me that I kept safely locked inside was the only physical photo that existed from the time before the fire. Before we'd lost her.

For a moment, the flames filled my vision. My throat burned from my screams, and my father's arms were iron bands around my chest.

"I didn't go back for her," I whispered. "I wanted to save her, but I didn't." The smoke seemed to choke my lungs, and my eyes stung.

Max curled two fingers beneath my chin, lifting my face to his so he could lock me in his intense black stare. I fell into the bottomless pools of his eyes, desperate to drown in them, to lose myself in him.

"There was nothing you could've done." His voice was roughened by his own pain.

I sniffled and swiped at the tears on my cheeks. "Sorry." I managed a watery apology. "I know you lost your mother too. It must have been hard for you."

His jaw hardened to granite. I pressed my palm against his cheek. His teeth stopped grinding beneath my tender touch, and the angry mask fell away. His brow furrowed with the pain that he kept so deeply buried.

"You couldn't have saved your mother," he said. "You're not responsible for her death." What was meant to be a comforting statement came out in a gravelly rasp. "I can't say the same. My mom died because I was too weak to save her."

I brushed my thumb over his cheekbone, commanding his attention and grounding him to me. "I'm sure that's not true," I countered softly. "You would've been a child when she died, right? What could you have possibly done?"

His eyes blazed, but he didn't pull away. "I watched them murder her," he snarled. "The Russians brutalized her before they killed her, and I watched. I didn't stop them."

I forgot how to breathe. "Max…" His name was a tight exhalation, and my eyes burned hotter.

His blind hatred and prejudice against Niko suddenly made awful sense, and I understood his misguided vendetta against my father with terrible clarity. If his family had told him that my dad had colluded with the Bratva—the criminal organization responsible for murdering his mother right in front of him—it was no wonder that he loathed Ron Fitzgerald.

The weight of the realization crushed my heart,

and the tears I shed were for him, for the agonized boy who'd endured unimaginable trauma and had blamed himself for over a decade.

"I was thirteen," he seethed. "Old enough to take on a man's responsibilities when it counted. I failed, and she died because of me."

Oh, Max.

"You're not responsible," I whispered, echoing the words he'd said to me.

I'd never realized how bound we were by similar pain. We both harbored a deep self-loathing, carrying guilt like a boulder on our shoulders. But where I'd hidden behind false smiles, Max had constructed his mask of rage to contain the terrible truth that we both held at our core.

I wasn't ready to let go of my guilt. I didn't know how to exist without it. If I released the strength it took to endure the strain, I might shatter into a million pieces.

He probably felt the same. I wouldn't push him to absolve himself, because I didn't want to break him.

Wordlessly, I pressed my forehead to his. He flinched when I made contact with his scar, so I caressed the right side of his face, allowing my fingers to slide over the damaged flesh for the first time. I wound them into his unruly curls, anchoring him to me. His massive body shuddered, and he leaned into my touch.

"Allie…" My name was a soft, pained groan.

A knock on my front door shattered the moment like a lightning strike. Max jolted away from me, and he was halfway to the foyer before I could blink. Confusion slowed my reaction time.

Who would be knocking on my door at this time of night? It had to be past ten o'clock by now.

Max's boots thundered over the tiles as he rushed to confront whoever was outside.

I surged to my feet and rushed after him, hastily buttoning my top. What if it was my dad? I couldn't imagine why he would come over right now, but it wouldn't be the first time he'd randomly stopped by to check on me.

My stomach dropped to the floor. I couldn't allow Max to see my dad. Especially not when he was so raw from his confession about witnessing his mother's murder. I'd seen the damage his massive fists could do to someone's face. If Max attacked my father, he would severely injure him.

I reached the foyer just as Max wrenched the door open. His low growl gave me pause, but I resolutely pressed forward.

"What the fuck are you doing here?" he demanded.

His hostile tone made my stomach knot, and I skidded to a stop just behind him. His muscular frame filled my doorway, blocking me with his bulk. I peeked over his shoulder, and my heart skipped a beat.

Max's sister stood on my front porch. The streetlight illuminated her sharp cheekbones, transforming her beautiful face into something savage and cruel. The physical similarities between her and Max had never been more apparent, with her harshly beautiful features and full lips twisted in a smirk. Her shark's eyes danced with cruel delight as they fixed on me.

"Hello, princess." Her white teeth flashed through the darkness, and her razor-sharp gaze cut back to Max. "Why didn't you tell me that sweet little Allie is the mayor's daughter?"

"Leave." The word was a barely intelligible snarl, and Max's big body practically vibrated with rage.

She lifted a slim shoulder in a casual shrug. "There's no need to be rude. I'm happy to leave with you, little brother. Father wants to see us."

All his muscles locked up tight. "Allie, go back inside."

Francesca gave him an exaggerated pout. "Don't be like that, Max. I'll leave your precious princess alone." She bared her shark-like smile at me. "You have nothing to fear from me."

My insides squirmed, but I forced myself to meet her glittering gaze. "Max is here at my invitation," I announced, lifting my chin in defiance. "You aren't. Please leave."

She turned her grin on Max. "Aw, she said *please*. So polite. Far too sweet for a brute like you. Come on, little brother. It's time to go."

Max's muscles coiled tight, ready to unleash violence to protect me. "I'm not leaving her. You shouldn't have come here, Francesca."

Her head canted to the side, her eyes gleaming as she waved behind her. "But I'm not the only one who came to pick you up. Our dear cousins are here. They'll drive us home, and we can all have a family meeting."

A black sedan waited at the curb. I could barely make out two dark silhouettes in the front seats.

My heart slammed against my ribcage as reality crashed down on me. I'd been so intent on convincing Max that he didn't scare me that I'd forgotten how frightening his relatives were. These people were mobsters. They'd committed the horrific, bloody crimes that'd given me nightmares during the week I'd spent poring over the Ferrara case files.

He was too young to have participated in those crimes. They weren't.

And they were waiting outside my house. They knew where I lived.

"Fine," Max ground out through gritted teeth. "I'll come with you. Just leave her alone."

"No!" I grabbed his forearm, desperate to keep him away from the monsters that waited for him in the dark. They might be his family, but they weren't kind to him. He wasn't safe with them. "Stay with me, Max."

His muscles flexed beneath my fingers, as though my weak hold was an iron shackle binding him in place.

"Aw, she's so cute," Francesca said in that awful singsong voice. "I bet our cousins would think so, too. Should I introduce them?"

"No!" Max barked, angling his body in front of mine so that I was completely blocked from their view. "I'm coming with you. Allie, stay inside. Lock the door behind me."

I couldn't let him leave with those monsters. My fingernails sank into his skin. "Please, don't go."

He wrenched his arm free, and my nails scored bright red lines into his flesh. He rounded on me, eyes blazing. "I'm leaving, Bambi." He spat the nickname in a warning tone.

He wanted me to know that I was putting myself in danger by confronting Francesca. The longer I kept him here, the worse things would get.

Francesca's tinkling laugh needled the base of my skull. "You have pet names for each other? Adorable."

He ignored her, focusing completely on me. His big hand cupped my cheek, his thick fingers sliding into my hair.

"I'll come back," he promised. "No matter what happens, I'll come back to you."

My heart tore open. What could possibly happen to him? What would his family do to him? They'd already inflicted mental torment by lying about my father's involvement with the Bratva, the organization that'd brutalized and murdered his mother right before his eyes. His sister clearly wielded words as a weapon, but what about his cousins? What were they capable of?

Bloody images from the case files filled my mind, and my eyes burned. His sensual lips brushed over my cheek, catching the tear that spilled over.

"I'll see you soon," he murmured in my ear, a fierce oath.

I swallowed hard and nodded. I dreaded the prospect of him leaving with his awful family, but he was choosing to go with them. Based on his sister's veiled threats, I believed he was protecting me. Max was strong, but I doubted he could take on the two men in the car and come out unscathed. If he went with them willingly, they wouldn't have a reason to hurt him.

I hoped I wasn't being naïve.

He'd told me so many times that I was naïve, and I'd bristled as though it was an insult. But faced with Francesca's delighted taunts, I realized I was completely out of my depth. Max knew it, and he wanted me to stay out of it. I would only be a liability to him if I insisted on involving myself further.

"I'll be waiting," I promised on a fierce whisper.

I wouldn't let Max go, no matter what. I cared about him too much to allow his family to take him from me. I had to trust that he could manage the situation without my interference.

He trusted me with his darkest secret. And I trusted him with my whole heart.

It fluttered in my chest at the realization. I'd never felt anything like this for any man. It was too soon, too wild, to call it love. But it was powerful and addictive enough that I never wanted it to end.

He pressed one last kiss to my forehead before pulling away with stilted, jerky movements, as though leaving me caused him physical pain.

"Lock the door," he commanded. "Now."

He kept his eyes on mine, refusing to leave until I was safely barricaded inside. I didn't want to lose sight of him for even a second, but I didn't have a choice. Max wouldn't be able to handle his family unless he believed I was safe.

I swallowed against the lump in my throat and shut the door between us, hiding him from my view. The heavy glide of the lock clicking into place slid between my ribs like a knife to the heart.

I rested my brow against the cool wood and listened to the heavy stomp of Max's boots as he retreated with his awful sister. The car started up and drove off, carrying the man I'd come to crave far away from me.

My chest squeezed, growing tighter with each of my racing heartbeats. Waiting for Max to safely return would be agony.

CHAPTER 21

*M*y heart hammered in my chest, and I curled my fingers to fists to hide their shaking. Adrenaline and rage ripped through my body, seeking a violent outlet.

Instead, I had to sit calmly in the back seat while my bitch of a sister watched me with a cruelly amused expression on her flawless face. I was hyper-aware of my cousins in the front seats. Their smug satisfaction flooded the car like noxious fumes. Everyone had been waiting to see me fail again. And falling for Alexandra Fitzgerald—our enemy's daughter—was an epic fuckup.

Aw, she's so cute. I bet our cousins would think so, too. Should I introduce them? The memory of Francesca's threat made my fury surge, and my fists clenched tighter.

My cousins were little more than beasts, caring only for power and twisted pleasure. They would rip Allie apart if my father let them off his leash.

A terrible image of Allie in pain screamed through my mind, ghosting over the familiar, nauseating memory of my mother's suffering before she'd finally been killed. My stomach lurched, and I swallowed against the acid burn in my throat.

"No one touches her," I ground out.

Francesca's light, hateful laugh floated through the car. "You really do like her. Pathetic."

"Why do you even care?" I demanded, even though I knew exactly why my relationship with Allie was forbidden.

My sister scoffed. "Don't pretend I'm an idiot. I didn't recognize your little princess when she came to the house, but that article about her in the *Times* told me who she was. Your girlfriend looks awfully cozy with Nikolai Ivanov. I'm surprised, Max. You were never good at sharing your toys."

Article? I had no idea what the fuck she was talking about, but clearly, whatever she'd read had revealed Allie's identity as Ron Fitzgerald's daughter. And her connection to *Niko.*

My gut twisted. This was far worse than anything I could've imagined. I'd only met Allie because I was trying to prove my worth, but somehow, I'd managed to fuck everything up. The evidence I'd wanted to gather in order to blackmail Fitzgerald was supposed to ensure my family's return to power. I would've been the one to usher in a new era of prosperity. I would've been a worthy heir, not a disgraced son.

"I followed you tonight, just to be sure," Francesca continued, as though my heart wasn't crumbling in my chest. "But I got bored of waiting for you to finish your little fuckfest. Sorry if I interrupted something important. I'm sure you haven't gotten laid in a while." She smirked at me. "Unless it's been long enough that you've been paying whores to get you off. Two years is a long time to be alone." Her voice softened with false pity. "But seriously, how did you ever get pretty Allie to accept a monster like you? How did you even meet?"

I ground my teeth together, refusing to give her a single word. My mind raced. How would I explain my relationship with Allie? There was no way I could tell my family the truth about how we'd met: that I'd kidnapped and interrogated her about her father's ties to the Bratva.

Not that they would be horrified by my actions. If I'd succeeded in getting the information I needed, I would've been celebrated by my family. Just like I'd planned.

But now, I couldn't let them know why I'd gotten close to Allie. It might make someone else decide that they could try again. And they would use much harsher methods of extracting answers.

"How could you be so stupid, Max?" The falsely cheery mask finally dropped, and Francesca glowered at me. "We're barely surviving. Uncle Tony is still in prison. And you're fucking the mayor's daughter? Do you want him to destroy what's left of us? We're not strong enough to withstand an attack right now. Not when Fitzgerald is still tight with scum like the Ivanovs. They would kill us all if he even suspected that you're defiling his precious princess."

I coiled tighter with each of her poisonous words. Because they were all true.

I'd endangered my entire family, and I'd endangered Allie. I couldn't seem to help breaking everything I touched, and now I'd committed my worst sin ever.

All my months of work stalking Fitzgerald were wasted. I couldn't even tell my father about my secret mission to restore our family to their rightful place. Everything was shattered beyond repair.

And worst of all, I'd put Allie at risk.

All along, I'd known that I shouldn't get close to

her. But I'd been too weak to resist. Francesca was right: no one had touched me since the fire.

But it was more than that. No one had ever looked at me like Allie did. Before I'd been scarred, women had only seen Paul Ferrara's heir, a dangerous and alluring conquest. Those who dared to approach me had been viciously beautiful and power-hungry. Even the women who wanted to be with me were a little bit scared of me.

I'd loved their respect, their awe and fear. I'd loved the hedonism of having no responsibilities but plenty of money to burn on whiskey and blow. While my father had been in prison, I'd been free to do whatever the fuck I wanted.

As soon as he came home, he'd made it clear that I was an entitled little shit. Unworthy of being his heir.

Now, my supposed friends had abandoned me. Family was all I had left, and I'd almost forsaken them for Allie.

We arrived at the house, and my stomach turned. I hadn't crossed the threshold in nearly two years. As soon as I'd healed from the most debilitating burns, I'd moved out on my own. Anything get away from the place where I'd been disciplined so harshly that I would bear the mark of my shame for the rest of my life.

"Fine," Francesca sighed. "Don't answer me. You can answer Father instead." She shook her head at me. "Why won't you let me help you, little brother? Do you always have to fuck up so bad?"

"You love when I fuck up," I spat.

She let out a little hum of agreement. "How else would I ever get Father to take me seriously? I'm just a woman, after all. But it's not my fault if his precious male heir is a failure." She spoke flippantly, but the words were edged with years of resentment.

She had to fight to prove herself every day. If she fucked up even once, our father would marry her off, using her to secure an alliance or net a good payday for the family. Her ruthlessness and resourcefulness—and my failures—were the only things that protected her from that fate.

I would've felt sorry for her if she weren't such a hateful bitch.

She opened her door, and I paused, jerking my chin in my cousins' direction. "I'm not coming inside unless John and Paulie do too."

Francesca released a derisive snort. "Don't worry. They won't go back and molest your girlfriend. No one wants that kind of conflict with Fitzgerald unless you force our hand. This meeting is for immediate family only." A single dark brow rose. "Father is waiting."

My gut twisted, and I barely suppressed a shudder.

Don't show weakness.

Snakes writhed inside me as I got out of the car and walked up the front steps. Dread crept over my consciousness, as though I was walking to the gallows.

The cavernous entry hall was eerily dim, the only illumination coming from lights shaped like sconces on either side of the front door. The two additional stories of open air above faded into shadow, and only the first third of the curving double staircase was visible.

I assumed Francesca had orchestrated the dramatic lighting. She knew how to suffocate some-one's psyche before they even approached our father.

Even though I was familiar with her psycholog-ical warfare, the creeping darkness was still unnerv-ing. Ghostly screams seemed to echo through the gloom, the memory of my own agony layering over my mother's cries for mercy. She'd begged for my worthless life, even as they'd brutalized her.

I managed to keep my shoulders relaxed until Francesca turned down the hallway leading to our father's study. My feet stalled out, concrete weights on the crimson carpet.

She shot me a smirk over her shoulder. She knew how that place decimated me.

Father knew it too.

My ruined face twisted with remembered agony, and for a moment, I smelled the sickly scent of burning flesh.

"Come on, little brother," Francesca urged in that terribly delighted, melodic tone. "You've already kept him waiting long enough."

I'd barely spoken a dozen words to my father since the incident. I only replied when he deigned to speak to me, and even then, there was only one acceptable response: "Yes, sir."

He'd made it clear that I had to earn his respect. It was the entire reason I'd come up with my plan to blackmail Fitzgerald.

Now all of that was ruined, and I was forced to face my worst nightmare.

My legs were leaden, but somehow, I managed to walk in Francesca's wake. It seemed to take an eternity to reach the study, but at the same time, we arrived far too quickly. She knocked on the dark wood door, and my father commanded us to enter. That single, clipped word shuddered through my system like a thunderclap.

Sweat beaded on my brow, and I clasped my

hands together behind my back to hide their shaking.

The uncontrollable physical responses to returning to this traumatic place made rage spark in my chest. I hated this weakness, the way my body betrayed me even when I wanted to be strong and composed.

Rage was familiar. Rage was strength.

I stoked the embers in my chest, allowing the anger to consume me. My trembling fingers stilled, and my back straightened with purpose. My mission to take down Fitzgerald and restore my rightful place in the family had seared me with purpose for nearly two years. I might've fucked that up beyond repair, but the strength of my fury would get me through this hell.

The door swung open, revealing the man I loathed and feared in equal measure. My father leaned back in his red leather armchair, swirling his whiskey in a crystal glass in a bored posture. His lips thinned, almost disappearing beneath his neatly trimmed, short black beard. A few flecks of silver glimmered at his temples, the first signs of advanced age only making him appear that much more severe. Prison had carved deep lines around his black eyes, and now, they were drawn like crags in a cliff face. His dark gaze punched my chest, knocking the air from my lungs.

I remembered the last time he'd glared at me with such disdainful loathing. He'd been drinking whiskey then, too. And so had I. But I'd been drunk on my own arrogance and alcohol, and when I'd dared to rail at him for his failures to protect our family, the viper had struck with terrible precision.

The feel of his hands on my neck, the heat of the flames licking my face as he inexorably shoved me into the fire...

My stomach lurched, and I tasted a copper tang on my tongue as I bit my cheek to ground myself with a little hit of pain. I couldn't allow myself to be sucked back into that terrible night. I had to stay alert and defend myself.

I had to defend Allie.

I thought of her peridot eyes, flashing like gemstones as she demanded my respect; the soft curve of her sensual lips as she told me she wasn't afraid of me; the heat of her lithe body melting beneath my demanding touch as I claimed every inch of her that she would yield to me.

I took a breath and stilled, settling fully into the present. I wouldn't allow my family to hurt her. No matter what I had to do, I would protect her.

"Your sister tells me that you're in a relationship

with Alexandra Fitzgerald." My father's drawl was soft and deceptively calm. "Our family is fractured. Your Uncle Tony is still in prison. Ron Fitzgerald would love an excuse to destroy what's left of us while we're critically weakened. He's still allied with the Bratva. With the men who murdered your mother." His voice rumbled with the hint of a growl on the last. For all of his cruelty, he'd loved my mother in his own way. He hated the men who'd taken her from us every bit as much as I did.

"Haven't you cost this family enough?" he spat. "You let the Russians kill your mother. You wasted years pissing away my money when you should've been rebuilding the family. And now, you're fucking our enemy's daughter. Explain yourself, Maximus."

Each of his accusations slammed into my wall of rage like a sledgehammer, seeking to shatter me. I gritted my teeth and drew my fury around me like a defensive shield. As long as I had the strength of my anger, I wouldn't break.

It allowed me the presence of mind to come up with an excuse to explain away my actions and protect Allie. If my family thought she meant nothing to me, they wouldn't have a reason to threaten her.

I squared my shoulders and met my father's glower head-on. "I started a relationship with

Alexandra to humiliate Fitzgerald," I explained in a calm, even voice. Not even a hint of my lie colored my tone. "She's an adult and can make her own choices independently of him. She's kind and sensitive, and she doesn't like that her dad tries to interfere in her life so much." I was betraying some of her secrets, but if that was the cost of her safety, I would give them to my family. "She likes me. If her father tries to break us up, his princess will resent him. I'm hitting him where it hurts most. She's the only family he has left."

My father cocked his head at me, stroking his beard. An agonizing minute of silence passed, and I fought the urge to squirm under his scrutiny. I clenched my fists behind my back and locked my shaking knees.

Don't show weakness.

"I appreciate that you were trying to hurt Fitzgerald," he finally allowed. "At least you're finally trying to help the family." He rested an elbow on the chair arm and leaned forward. I felt his menace crash over me like a wave of condemnation. "But it was a stupid fucking plan. If you damage Fitzgerald's relationship with his daughter, do you think he's just going to take it on the chin? No. He'll come after what's left of us. You will end this relationship, and you will pray that she's not stupid enough to breathe a word about it to her dad."

"But he won't want to do that, will you, Max?" My sister chimed in with her falsely sympathetic voice. "You might have approached her in order to humiliate her father, but you truly care about her. I saw how you looked at her. You were ready to fight our cousins to protect her. She's compromised your loyalties. I think you might even love her."

Her hateful words pierced my heart. Yes, I was falling for Allie. She *saw* me in a way no one else ever had, and I was addicted to the way she looked at me —like I wasn't a monster. I craved her like I'd never wanted any woman. She was the only person who'd shown me even a shred of true kindness since my mother had died.

She understood my pain and my guilt in a way no one else could. No one else had even bothered to try.

But Allie had insisted on knowing me. She was stubborn and infuriating and absolutely perfect.

My father's eyes narrowed. "Is this true? Do you care for this girl?"

"No."

Everyone heard the lie drop like a stone between us.

His lips pressed to a thin line, twisting as though he'd bitten something sour. "End it." The sharp command lashed me like a whip. "End it, or I swear to god, I'll send your cousins to pay her a visit. Your little humiliation play will only draw Fitzgerald's ire without truly landing a blow. I don't want to draw his attention to us just yet, but if you won't let her go, I'll send him a message he'll understand.

"The Ferraras are done cowering and licking our wounds. If you choose to put his daughter in the line of fire, that's your prerogative. With any luck, you'll be the head of this family one day, and you'll have to learn to make hard decisions." Black eyes bored into my soul. "End it, or the girl suffers. Your choice."

I swallowed the acid in my throat and offered the only answer I could: "Yes, sir."

CHAPTER 22

ALLIE

My phone chimed with a text just before Max knocked on my door: *It's me.*

I jolted to my feet from where I'd been curled up on my couch, consumed with worry for him. He'd been gone for more than an hour, and terrible, bloody scenes had played through my mind.

I rushed to the door and flung it open, revealing Max's familiar, shadowy form. I threw myself at him, exhaling a soft sob of relief as I wrapped my arms around his shoulders and hugged him close. I pressed my face against his chest and breathed in his salt-kissed leather scent, listening to the heavy beat of his heart beneath my ear.

Max was safe. He was here. And he was holding

me like I was the only thing in the world that mattered.

I lifted my face to his, tipping my head back to invite his fierce kiss. I wanted him to consume me. I wanted to wrap myself up in him and feel that he was okay.

But he didn't bend down to claim my offered kiss. Instead, every line of his massive body went taut, and he released me from his iron embrace. I clung on to him, refusing to allow him to put distance between us.

My heart sank as he pulled away. I clutched him tighter.

"What's wrong?" I asked, my voice small. My chest tightened with the early symptoms of rejection. I forced down a breath and refused to acknowledge them.

His strong hands wrapped around my shoulders, and for a moment, my heart leapt. But instead of pulling me close, he pried me away from his hard body, holding me at arm's length.

"We're done," he announced, his voice flat and cold.

"What?" I asked on a little puff of air.

I shook my head. Something must've happened with his family to make him say such an awful thing. I'd welcomed him into my heart. I'd let him touch me in ways no other man had. His soul called to mine.

I wouldn't let him go.

"Tell me what happened," I pleaded. "Something's wrong."

His jaw firmed, and his head tipped back, obscuring his features with that awful, skull-like shadow. "Yes," he agreed, his tone clipped. "Everything about this is wrong. We can't be together."

I clutched at him, struggling to pull him closer. He held me fast, stubbornly maintaining the wall of air between our bodies. It might as well have been constructed of solid concrete.

"What did they say to you?" I demanded, defiant anger sparking on his behalf. His awful family wouldn't break us up. Had they done something to him? Had they hurt him?

My hands roved over his torso, searching for injuries. His muscles flexed beneath my touch, and he released a low, warning growl.

My fingers curled into his shirt, holding on tight. I wouldn't let him slip away.

"They reminded me of who I really am, Bambi."

The nickname was suddenly cold and cruel, and I flinched as though he'd slapped me.

I pressed on, desperation gnawing at my insides. "I know who you are," I insisted hotly. "I don't know what they said to you, but you're not a monster, Max."

"Yes, I am!" he thundered. "You're a naïve little girl, and you just want to stay ignorant. You don't know the first thing about me."

"That's bullshit," I seethed, my eyes burning. "You're just being cruel to push me away for some reason. It won't work. They did something to hurt you. Talk to me," I begged.

He went utterly still. "You think I'm not a monster? My family killed your mother. I knew, and I didn't tell you because I wanted you."

"What?" The word was breathless, as though he'd punched me in the chest.

"For once in your goddamn life, listen to me, Bambi. I'll speak slowly so you understand." He sneered, and something withered inside me. "You've never wanted to hear this, but your father is corrupt. When he brought down the indictments against my family, they punished him for it. They murdered your mom, and he covered it up to make it look like an accident."

Something was crumbling inside my chest. I shook my head weakly. "My mother died in a fire."

"You think it's your fault that she died because you didn't run back into that fire to save her. But there was nothing you could've done. She was already dead," he replied, cold as ice. "Your father started the fire to cover up her murder. He didn't want anyone asking uncomfortable questions. There was the election to think about." The words dripped from his sensual lips like poison. "And then, his Russian friends killed my mom in retribution."

Before I could even begin to process the awful things he was saying, he landed the final blow. "You're lucky my family reminded me who I really am. I would've fucked you. The blood of your mother's murderers runs in my veins, and I would've taken everything you offered me without saying a word about it. I am a monster, Allie." His voice rasped on my name.

Tears fell down my cheeks in hot streams, and I reeled back from him. His hands tightened on my shoulders, clasping me to him reflexively.

I couldn't take this. I'd shared my deepest pain, my worst vulnerability with him, and he was using it to shred me. I'd been able to handle it when he'd spoken his insane lies about my father's involvement with the Bratva, but this was too much. He'd located my most painful secret—that I felt responsible for my mother's death—and he was punching it with words that were more brutal than his fists could ever be.

"I trusted you!" I shoved his chest, recoiling from

him. "Let me go," I choked out, my demand hitching on a sob.

He tugged me closer, and his beautiful face twisted into something desperate and hungry. "Allie..."

"You're right." My voice shook with tears. "You are a monster, Max." I wrenched myself free from his grip.

He let me go, and I stumbled back, throwing a hand against the wall in my foyer to catch myself.

He reached out as though to steady me.

"Don't touch me!" I shrieked.

His hand clenched to a fist and slowly dropped to his side. His dark eyes burned, twin white flames flickering over the bottomless black expanses.

"We're done." His voice was heavy with absolute truth. He turned sharply on his heel and stalked away.

He didn't demand that I lock my door before he left. He didn't promise to protect me from anyone who might be lurking in the shadows.

He abandoned me.

Something at the center of my chest shattered into a thousand sharp slivers. They pierced my lungs, robbing my breath and lancing me with unendurable pain.

I had put my heart in Max Ferrara's hands, and he had crushed it.

Thank you for reading RAPTURE & RUIN! I hope you loved this first installment in Max and Allie's tumultuous romance. Their story continues in TORMENT & TEMPTATION!

ALSO BY JULIA SYKES

Rapture & Ruin

Rapture & Ruin

Torment & Temptation

Sins & Salvation

The Captive Series

Sweet Captivity

Claiming My Sweet Captive

Stealing Beauty

Captive Ever After

Pretty Hostage

Wicked King

Ruthless Savior

The Impossible Series

Impossible

Savior

Rogue

Knight

Mentor

Mafia Ménage Trilogy

Mafia Captive

The Daddy and The Dom

Theirs to Protect

Made in the USA
Middletown, DE
21 September 2021